HARBINGERS 15

Fairy

Angela Hunt

Alton Gansky, Bill Myers, and Jeff Gerke

D1529042

Published by Amaris Media International in conjunction with CreateSpace.

Copyright © 2016 Angela Hunt

Cover Design: Angela Hunt

Photo credits: © Igor Mejzes – fotolia.com
   © Viktoriagavril—fotolia.com.

All rights reserved. No part of this book may be reproduced, stored in a retrieval system, or transmitted in any form or by any other means—electronic, mechanical, photocopy, recording, or any other—except for brief quotations in printed reviews, without prior permission from the publisher.

ISBN-13: 978-1537051024
ISBN-10: 1537051024

For more information, visit us on Facebook:
https://www.facebook.com/pages/Harbingers/705107309586877

or *www.harbingersseries.com*.

HARBINGERS

A novella series by
Bill Myers, Jeff Gerke, Angela Hunt,
and Alton Gansky

In this fast-paced world with all its demands, the four of us wanted to try something new. Instead of the longer novel format, we wanted to write something equally as engaging but that could be read in one or two sittings—on the plane, waiting to pick up the kids from soccer, or as an evening's read.

We also wanted to play. As friends and seasoned novelists, we thought it would be fun to create a game we could participate in together. The rules were simple:

Rule #1

Each of us will write as if we were one of the characters in the series:

Bill Myers will write as Brenda, the street-hustling tattoo artist who sees images of the future.

Frank Peretti will write as the professor, the atheist ex-priest ruled by logic.

Jeff Gerke will write as Chad, the mind reader with devastating good looks and an arrogance to match.

Angela Hunt will write as Andi, the brilliant-but-geeky young woman who sees inexplicable patterns.

Alton Gansky will write as Tank, the naïve, big-hearted jock with a surprising connection to a healing power.

Rule #2

Instead of the five of us writing one novella together (we're friends but not crazy), we would write it like a TV series. There would be an overarching storyline into which we'd plug our individual novellas, with each story written from our character's point of view.

If you're keeping track, this is the order:

Harbingers 1—*The Call*—Bill Myers
Harbingers 2—*The Haunted*—Frank Peretti
Harbingers 3—*The Sentinels*—Angela Hunt
Harbingers 4—*The Girl*—Alton Gansky

Volumes 1-4 omnibus: *Cycle One: Invitation*

Harbingers 5—*The Revealing*—Bill Myers
Harbingers 6—*Infestation*—Frank Peretti
Harbingers 7—*Infiltration*—Angela Hunt
Harbingers 8—*The Fog*—Alton Gansky

Volumes 5-8 omnibus: *Cycle Two: Mosaic*

Harbingers 9—*Leviathan*—Bill Myers
Harbingers 10—*The Mind Pirates*—Frank Peretti
Harbingers 11—*Hybrids*—Angela Hunt
Harbingers 12—*The Village*—Alton Gansky

Volumes 9-12 omnibus: *Cycle Three: The Probing*

Harbingers 13—*Piercing the Veil*—Bill Myers
Harbingers 14—*Home Base*—Jeff Gerke
Harbingers 15—*Fairy*—Angela Hunt
Harbingers 16: ??—Alton Gansky

There you have it, at least for now. We hope you'll find these as entertaining in the reading as we did in the writing.

Bill, Frank, Jeff, Angie, and Al

Chapter 1

"What is this?" I picked up the box Chad had just tossed into my lap.

"The Smartech Simultalk 36G Wireless Communication system," he said, tossing identical boxes to Brenda, Daniel, and Tank. "Now whenever we're out in the field, we won't have to rely on cell phones or extra-sensory perception. We'll rely on this state-of-the art professional communication system."

I opened the box and pulled out a manual and two devices—an earpiece and a mouthpiece.

"I saw Katie Perry wearing something like this the other day," Brenda said, tossing her manual aside. "Looked cool."

I bent the wire attached to the mouth piece—a slender plastic tube—and hooked it over my ear. "Did I do this right?"

Chad nodded. "Looks great—of course, anything would look great on—"

"Got it," I interrupted, cutting him off. "And this little plastic thing goes into my ear?"

"Just like a hearing aid." Chad demonstrated with his earpiece. "See? Practically invisible."

"The mouth piece isn't," Brenda pointed out.

"But that's the beauty of the Smartech Simultalk," Chad said, grinning. "You can slip that little mouthpiece anywhere, as long as it's within thirty-six inches of your face. You could put it in your collar, hide it in the cuff of a sleeve, even slip it in your belt. It's going to pick up any sound in your vicinity."

I glanced at Tank, who hadn't said much. He wore a frown the size of Texas and was still pulling pieces out of his box. "And why do we need this?" he asked.

"Communication, my man," Chad said, flashing that Ultra-bright smile. "An unlimited number of radios can be added to the system in talk or listen-only mode. We can talk simultaneously without wires—and this is a lot less clunky than the old systems where you had to wait for one person to finish before another person could begin."

"Hang on." I pointed to the box. "It says here that we can have one-way or full duplex operation at the touch of a button. What button?"

"Look in the bottom of your box."

I pulled out a couple of pieces of cardboard, then found a black plastic gizmo about the size of a pack of playing cards. The thing featured an antenna and two buttons on top, but not much else.

"I'll teach you noobs how to use it," Chad continued, oozing arrogance with every smile. "In fact, why don't we have a dry run this afternoon? We can walk through the hotel and practice to test the limits of the system. After all, we wouldn't want to head out to some dangerous assignment without knowing what we're doing."

Brenda tipped her head back and laughed, and even Tank joined in.

"What's so funny?" Chad looked from them to me. "Care to let me in on the joke?"

I chuckled. "The thing is, Chad, we've gone out every time without knowing what we're doing, and we've survived."

"Without you," Brenda said, arching a brow.

"Then maybe it's time to try a new approach." He looked around the circle, his eyes serious. "You guys have had some close calls, and most of the time you've been playing defense. Maybe it's time to up the ante. Learn some new plays. Go on the offensive for a change."

"Mixed metaphors aside," I said, resisting the temptation to roll my eyes, "I do think these communication gizmos are a good idea. I hate it when we get separated, and if these can help, great."

"And what's with this *you guys* stuff?" Tank asked, looking at Chad. "For better or worse, you're one of us now. So make that a *we*, all right?"

I looked away, unable to stand the sight of Tank being nice and gentlemanly while most of the time I wanted to slap Chad upside the head. He was smart, he had gifts, but we had to pay for those gifts by tolerating his smarminess, his sexist comments, and his all-round obnoxiousness.

I caught Daniel grinning at Chad as if they shared some kind of private joke. I wasn't sure, but I had a feeling those two were communicating on some level the rest of us couldn't reach. Daniel had never been exceptionally verbal, but he and Chad had become as close as peas in a pod, probably because Chad had been popping into his brain or something to tell him bedtime stories every night . . .

I'd have to speak to Brenda. Chad couldn't possibly be a good influence on an impressionable boy.

"All right—I agree that we need to start playin' offense," Brenda said. "How do we do that?"

She looked at me, I looked at Tank, and Tank looked at Chad—who looked at Daniel. Daniel nodded soberly. "Wait," he said. "Wait for

Watchers."

"There." Chad smiled, looking incredibly pleased with himself. "We wait for the Watchers to give us a clue. And in the meantime, we practice using our comms."

I blew out a breath and caught Brenda's eye. She made a face that seemed to say *Can you believe this?*, but since she had no better ideas, she didn't say anything.

Neither did I.

* * *

"This is Andi." I adjusted my comms mouthpiece, then slipped a straw into the iced tea the waitress had just brought me. "Is anyone listening?"

Chad had promised that the operation of our comm units would be simple. All the remote devices continually monitored whichever unit we designated as the master. To talk, we simply pressed the second button on our transceiver, then waited for someone to respond. Simple, right?

"Andi?" Tank's booming voice filled my ear, causing me to wince. "Are you still in the hotel?"

"I'm in the downstairs restaurant. Where are you?"

He laughed. "I'm at the airport ticket counter. But you sound like you're right around the corner."

I smiled. Considering that the hotel was part of the airport's D terminal, he *was* right around the corner. Sort of.

"That's good. Brenda, Daniel—where are you guys?"

I heard nothing, then Brenda's exasperated sigh filled my ears. "We're at the airport, too—at the ice cream counter in Terminal B. Daniel was hungry."

I smiled. So far, so good. At least we knew the comms worked. "Chad?" I asked. "Where are you?"

No answer.

"Maybe he's out of range," Tank said.

"Or chasing some babe," Brenda suggested.

I groaned. "I hope he catches one," I said. "Someone who'll give him a piece of her—"

"Chad here, at Dallas central. Good to hear all of you."

I exhaled in guilty relief. He was fine. And he hadn't been chasing a babe or one of the ghasts we'd met when we first moved into our suites at the Grand Hyatt. I never wanted to meet another one of those creepy things.

"Were you takin' a nap?" Brenda asked. "You were awfully slow on the uptake."

"Sorry, guys—had to answer the door. We got a special delivery package."

A premonition nipped at the back of my neck. "Who's it from?"

"It's addressed to you, Andi, but the bellman let me sign for it since you didn't answer your door. Should I open it?"

"Wait," I said, signaling the waitress. "I think we should open it together."

"Suit yourself," Chad answered. "I'll be waiting in my love nest."

"Excuse me?"

"My suite. So get yourself up here post haste."

"We're on our way."

Chapter 2

Twenty minutes later, we had all gathered around the giant television in Chad's suite. I had opened the box and pulled out a letter and a DVD in a plain cardboard sleeve. Chad sat on the floor by the TV, and lifted his hand for the DVD. After slipping it in the slot, he found a seat on the sofa next to Daniel.

We all leaned forward as the black screen filled with two words: THE WATCHERS. Then a voice spoke: "Greetings, team! We hope you are well and rested since your move into the hotel. If you have any problem with the accommodations, or with anything on your journeys, you should memorize our email address:

help@watchers.com. We monitor the site continually, and we'll get help to you as soon as we can."

"A help line." Brenda's mouth curved in a smile. "We coulda used one of those when we first got together. What took 'em so long?"

"Be grateful," I murmured, my eyes intent on the screen. "At least we have a sponsor now."

I couldn't help but wonder why the so-called Watchers were so secretive with us. We were supposed to be on the same team, so why would they be unwilling to show their faces? Would be nice to put a face to the voice, but apparently full disclosure wasn't part of the plan.

"We've hired a plane for you," the resonant baritone continued. "It's a private jet leaving from Hanger 44 tomorrow morning at 10:00 a.m. Be on time, please, and dress in comfortable clothes and shoes. You might have to do a bit of walking. You should also bring your communications system and the video camera."

"What video camera?" Tank asked.

Chad grinned. "No worries—I have it."

Of course he did.

"One more thing," the speaker said. "You'll need your passports. We are sending you to meet Mr. Benedicto Prospero, a television broadcaster and celebrity in his homeland. He speaks English, so you should have no trouble communicating with him. If you speak any Spanish at all, however, it might be useful to brush up on your skills. You might need to interview several people on your journey."

"So where are we goin'?" Brenda growled. "Half the world speaks Español."

"Mr. Prospero is going to show you something unusual," the unnamed speaker continued. "Your mission is to verify the object, determine where it came from, and see if you can establish its purpose. The task may be more difficult than we anticipate, but do your best and send a report when you return. Take photographs, record video, and gather any evidence you can transport home. And if you have any difficulty meeting your contact, you might try asking him about the fairy."

The voice—whoever it was—paused. "Thank you for your willingness to serve in our effort, and Godspeed. Enjoy Mexico City."

We heard a second of silence, a short hiss, and then nothing.

Chad cracked a smile. "Sort of ripping off Mission Impossible, aren't they?"

"Yeah, maybe," I admitted. "But I didn't hear anything about the DVD self-destructing."

"What's this about a fairy?" Brenda asked. "Compared to the monsters we've encountered lately, fairies sound like a nice change."

"Yeah." I parked my chin in my palm and smiled. "When I was a kid, I had a fairy costume. Lots of tulle and sparkles and a magic wand."

"Wings?" Chad asked.

"Oh, for sure. Can't be a fairy without beautiful wings."

"Mexico City." Tank's eyes widened. "Isn't that a humongous place?"

"It is," I said, trying to remember what little I knew about Mexico's capital. I unfolded the letter from the package and skimmed it. "This letter doesn't give us any more information—it has Benedicto Prospero's name and address, and reminds us to send a report when we get back. It also reminds us that we can get help if we send an email."

"I don't get the fairy thing," Tank said. "Sounds crazy."

"Maybe it's some kind of code," Brenda said, shrugging. "A secret password."

"Like Tinkerbell," Daniel suggested.

Brenda groaned. "He's been watching old Disney movies. *Peter Pan* is his latest fave."

"You know, we ought to be able to find out something from that email addy," Chad said, crossing his arms. "Or am I the only one bright enough to be curious about our benefactors?"

"I'm curious," I said, "but not so curious that I want to go snooping in the business of people who are clearly on our side. If they don't want to give us more information, maybe we should respect that."

"It's just a matter of looking up watchers.com and seeing who owns the domain," Chad said. "Nothing wrong with that."

Tank laughed. "I don't know much about computers, but these people are too smart to make it easy."

"Yeah," Brenda agreed. "I'm just grateful they're on our side. If they don't want to provide life histories, I'm good with that."

"And they've given us a way to ask for help." I thumped the folded letter against my palm. "That's amazing."

"Agreed," Brenda said, looking at Daniel. "But is anyone else concerned that they seem pretty sure we're gonna need it?"

* * *

We landed at a private airport outside Mexico City around lunch time—and I was glad the trip didn't take longer.

When Chad met us downstairs, his eyes were watery and his nose red. "I hab a cobe in my nose," he said, wearing a face like a beaten dog's. He shuffled over to me. "Wanna kiss me and make it better?"

I recoiled from the suggestion and backed away from his germs. "Are you really sick? Should you stay home?"

"I'm all right," Chad said, holding a finger under his nose. "I—I—" He sneezed. "Sorry 'bout that. I should be fine in a little while. Just took a heavy duty antihistamine."

"Great," I said, leading the way toward the waiting cab. "We'll be investigating and you'll be asleep."

As I expected, Chad did nod off during the flight. I hoped he'd wake with a clear head and be fully functional, but with Chad, I wasn't sure what "fully functional" was.

He wasn't the only one with physical issues. For the last hour of the flight, Tank's stomach growled so loudly that we could hear it rumbling throughout the cabin. At first, I was embarrassed for the big guy, but when he started talking back to his stomach, it became a running gag. "Who's the big bad on this adventure?" Brenda joked. "A ghost? A flying sphere? No—it's Cowboy's belly!"

I didn't want to laugh, but when Daniel cracked up, I had to chuckle. Poor Tank.

"I had a big breakfast," he said, his face drooping in a woeful expression. "Stack of pancakes, scrambled eggs, six sausage links, grits, orange juice, and biscuits with sausage gravy. I thought that would hold me over 'til lunchtime, but I guess flyin' makes me hungry."

Brenda looked up from her sketchbook and turned to Daniel. "If you plannin' to eat like that when you get bigger, I'm gonna need a second job."

Daniel grinned and looked out the window. While Brenda was distracted, I leaned over the back of my seat to get a peek at what she'd been sketching. The dark figure on her page was vaguely human, with spindly limbs, a knobby skull, jagged teeth, and wings.

I'd seen prettier pictures.

"Had a good look?"

I looked up, my cheeks flushing hot, and met Brenda's gaze. "I was just, um, wondering what we might be heading into. That—" I pointed at her sketchpad—"doesn't look friendly."

"It's probably nothing." She shrugged and flipped the lid of her sketchbook. "I dreamed about it last night, but like I said, Daniel's been into Disney films lately—he's catching up on all the stuff he missed while he was locked up in that psychiatric hospital. I figure that monster is a mix of Maleficent and a dragon, with a little Tinkerbell thrown in for good measure."

"I hope you're right."

We taxied to a private hanger and woke up Chad, then the pilot gave us the all-clear for grabbing our luggage and heading out. We had packed lightly—most of us brought only one small bag or backpack, and we were wearing jeans, short-sleeved shirts, and sneakers. Daniel was wearing a *Walking Dead* tee-shirt, much to Brenda's chagrin.

"I tried to talk him out of buying it," she had told me earlier. "I said nobody wanted to look at zombies and stuff. But then he said the zombies were nuthin' compared to things we'd seen, and he had me there. What could I say?" She shrugged. "Anyway, he knows that stuff is make-believe."

Yet here we were, about to drive into Mexico City to investigate something else that might be make-believe. But considering everything the Watchers had done to prepare us for the trip, something in me doubted that we'd be seeing a fake. Still, we had to keep our eyes, ears, and minds open.

We grabbed our bags and headed into small office, where we had to go show our passports. Getting into Mexico was easy, but we hit a glitch in customs. For some reason, a guy at the customs area opened our bags as we entered the area, then stood behind them with his arms crossed and his face somber.

We waited for Chad, who was moving slower than usual, then motioned for him to join us on a white line painted on the cement floor. The surly customs agent took Chad's bag when he arrived, then opened it and glared at us. "You are bringing forbidden items into Mexico," he snapped, looking as though he wanted to send us straight back home. "You will be arrested and spend the night in jail."

Tank's mouth spread in a good-ol'-boy smile. "Now, hang on a minute, buddy," he began, but the man silenced Tank by moving to the big guy's suitcase. I was afraid he was going to reach in and pull out a bag of crack cocaine or something else he'd planted, but instead he pulled out the box containing Tank's comms gear.

"What is this?" the customs agent snarled.

Tank looked at Chad, and for the first time since I'd met him, Chad appeared at a loss for words. "That is um, a state-of-the-art wireless communications unit," he said. "You know—like a walkie-talkie."

The agent's frown only deepened. "This is forbidden. This violates international order C-475 regarding wireless communications over unsecured frequencies."

"That is perfectly legitimate equipment," Chad argued. "Made by an international company who must certainly sell goods in Mexico."

The man dropped Tank's comms unit on the table, then reached into my bag, Brenda's, Daniel's, and Chad's. In each case, he pulled out the comms unit and dropped it on the table. When we had finished, we were looking at a heap of wires, plastic battery packs, and a couple of instruction manuals. "Confiscated," the man said, his face twisting in an oily smile. He scooped up all the units and left through a swinging door, leaving our bags on the table and us standing behind the white line.

I turned to Chad. "I thought you said those things were good."

"They're the best," he said. "Navy Seals use them."

"Maybe that's the problem," Tank said. "Maybe it's top secret technology, and the Mexicans want to get their hands on it."

"Anyone ever heard of international order C-475?" Brenda asked. "Maybe he made it up. They're going to learn our secrets by studying our gizmos."

"Maybe," Chad said, looking bemused. "Or maybe that guy's a ghast, and this has all been part of a plot to stop us. I could hit him over the head with a chair to see what happens—"

"Why don't you just pop into his brain?" Brenda suggested, her tone sharp. "Save us all a lot of trouble."

Chad blew out a breath. "Reading his thoughts wouldn't help me. I don't speak Spanish. Besides, I think those pills have somehow short-circuited things. My brain feels like it's full of fog."

Brenda burst out laughing and I tried to regain some level of control over the situation.

"Let's not hit anyone or play with their brains." I tapped Chad's arm. "Let's just get our stuff and leave as soon as we can."

A moment later the customs agent returned, empty-handed. He studied our group for a moment, then stepped back and slipped his hands into his pockets. "You are free to go."

We hurried forward to claim our bags and get out of the airport before he changed his mind.

I had hoped our bosses would have a hired car waiting, but apparently the people who thought of everything hadn't thought about having a taxi waiting. Instead we hitched a ride on a couple of airport golf carts, went to the main terminal, and hailed a minivan cab at the curb.

I settled my bag under my feet and tried to relax. At least we had made it to Mexico City.

Chapter 3

Our cab driver looked at us and frowned. "No speak-e Ingles."

All of the others looked at me. "Okay. Um." I wracked my brain as I fumbled for the letter in my purse. *"Queremos ir aquí."* Not having the faintest idea if I'd said the right thing, I handed the paper with Benedicto Prospero's address to our cab driver. He squinted at it, and for a moment I was afraid he'd tell us he'd never heard of the place.

"Ah." The man nodded at the paper, then

handed it back to me. "OK. We go."

I leaned back in the seat and looked at Brenda, who sat with Daniel on the bench seat behind me. She shook her head, grinning, and Daniel seemed thrilled by all the hustle and bustle of the airport.

"I don't know about this one," Tank said, turning to look at me from the front passenger seat. "I'm gettin' a bad feelin'."

"You always got a bad feelin'," Brenda said, slipping her arm around Daniel's thin shoulders. "Relax, Cowboy. We're in the land of siestas and margaritas. Of sombreros and—"

"Chupacabras," Tank interrupted. He lowered his voice and turned, cupping his hand to whisper. "Meanin' no disrespect to the country, but haven't you noticed that an awful lot of superstitious stuff comes out of Mexico? I've heard all kinds of things about weepin' paintings and bleedin' statues, and that stuff always seems to come from Mexico or South America. Plus, you've got them Aztecs and their human sacrifices—"

"The Aztecs are long gone, big guy," Brenda said. "And you're probably the last name on any list of possible human sacrifices."

I leaned forward to pat Tank's arm. Brenda and Chad teased him all the time, but I couldn't bring myself to do it. Probably because I knew he had feelings for me (whatever they were, I tried to keep them at bay) and because I knew he was all heart beneath that brawny exterior.

"We're going to be fine," I assured him. "After all, the assignment seems fairly straightforward. After all, no one has tried to kill us yet."

I meant that last bit as a joke, but Tank took it seriously. "I'm not so sure about that." He lifted a bushy brow. "That customs guy looked like he was ready to shoot anyone who spoke out of turn."

"Pfft." Brenda waved the matter away. "That's history. We'll just get some more of those comms thingies and use 'em on our next trip."

As Tank and Chad began to argue about whether people from Mexico were more superstitious than Americans, I looked out the window and watch the country slide by. The international airport was fully as modern as anything in the United States, and the freeway into the capital city was crowded with fast-moving cars. Once we reached the city, we drove along streets filled with skyscrapers that made the trees beneath them look like miniature decorations. "The city is really beautiful," I said to anyone who would listen. "I don't know what I was expecting, but these buildings are architecturally stunning."

The driver must have caught the gist of what I was saying, because he began to point out various buildings. I didn't understand much his description, but as he shifted into the right hand lane, he pointed at one building and said, "*La estación de televisión es dentro de este edificio.*"

"Television station," I repeated. "*Si. Muchas gracias.*"

"We're here?" Brenda asked.

"I think so."

The driver pulled into an underground parking lot, then turned into an area that would allow him to drop us off and exit without having to park. "*Es un televisión estación?*" I asked.

The driver nodded, so I pulled out my wallet, only to discover that I had completely forgotten about the change in currency. "Um . . ." I showed him three U.S. twenties. "Es okay?"

He grinned. "*Muy okay.*" As everyone else piled out of the minivan, he took the money and gave me a blank receipt and drove off.

Chad, Tank, Brenda, Daniel and I stood in front of the elevator without a clue as to what we should do next. "Well," Chad said, pushing the elevator button, "every building has a lobby, and every lobby should have a receptionist or a list of tenants. Let's find Señor Prospero."

The doors opened and we shuffled inside the elevator car, making room for each other and our luggage.

"Prospero," Chad mused as the doors slid shut. "*Prosperity.* Coincidence, do you think?"

I shrugged. "I've never met the man."

"Well, hold onto your hats," Brenda said as the elevator began to rise. "Because I think we're about to."

* * *

Benedicto Prospero was not listed among the building tenants, but we did spot five television stations: XEW, XHTV, XEQ, XHOF, XAT, and XEIPN. A couple of the stations were owned by Grupo Televisa and TV Azteca, the other by Grupo Prospero.

"There you go," I said, pointing to XAT. "Either our guy owns the station or one of his relatives does."

"Could be coincidence," Chad said.

"The odds are against it." I flashed him a brief smile, then led the way back the elevator. "Going up, anyone?"

We exited on the forty-fourth floor, home to XAT and the offices of Grupo Prospero. With a confidence I didn't exactly feel, I walked through a pair of glass doors and up to an ebony reception desk that stood at the center of a two-story lobby.

"*Hola*," I said, hoping the receptionist spoke English. "*Me amigos y yo de donde los Estados Unidos. Quiero*—we want to see—señor Benedicto Prospero. We believe he'll want to see us."

The pretty receptionist lifted a brow. "Was he expecting you today?"

She understood me! I slumped in relief. "I'm not sure. But it's important that we see him."

She looked at me, an uncertain smile on her face. "I'm sorry, but if you do not have an appointment, I cannot let you see Señor Prospero. He is a very busy man."

"But we've come all the way from Dallas."

"Texas," Tank added. "In the U.S. of A."

The receptionist smiled. "Señor Prospero is in the studio this afternoon and will not be finished recording until late. If you want to come back tomorrow—"

I broke eye contact with her when Brenda elbowed me. Someone was moving on floor above—a middle-aged man in a dress shirt and tie, with paper towels or something tucked over his collar. The guy had apparently just come out of makeup, which meant he was about to go into the studio—

"Señor Prospero? Benedicto Prospero?" I called.

The gentleman did not look happy to be interrupted. "Como?" he said, glancing down at us.

"*Con permiso, señor*—my friends and I would like to talk to you about . . . the fairy." I spoke the last word reluctantly, knowing that I stood in a public place, but we all saw his countenance change at my words. The man who would have brushed us off without hesitation went pale, and the hand he placed on the railing trembled slightly.

"You know . . . about that?"

"Yes. We were sent here to investigate it."

"By whom?"

"Please, señor—may we speak in private?"

He glanced quickly left and right, then pressed

his lips together. After a moment, he seemed to come to a decision. "Conchita, show them the way to the staircase, please. Tell everyone I am not to be interrupted for the next hour."

* * *

We climbed the stairs and met Señor Prospero in a hallway. Keeping his voice low, he led us to a conference room, then indicated that we should drop our luggage against the wall. When we had lightened our load, he crooked a finger and led us into a luxurious office with lots of open space, gorgeous leather guest chairs, and a desk about as wide as a barn door.

I took a moment to introduce everyone. "We work for an organization called the Watchers," I said. "I can't say much about them, but—"

"I know who they are," Señor Prospero said.

While I blinked in amazement, he opened his top desk drawer and pulled out a Bible. Flipping to the center, he ran his finger over the text, then grunted. "*Aqui esta. Para esto ha sido decretado por los observadores—*"

"We don't speak Spanish," Brenda told him.

Prospero nodded. "Ah. Forgive me. 'For this has been decreed by the *watchers*, it is commanded by the holy ones, so that everyone may know that the Most High rules over the kingdoms of the world.' From the book of Daniel, chapter four."

The man looked up as if his explanation should satisfy us, but I could make no sense of it. I looked at Tank, our official Bible gee whiz kid, and he looked as confused as I felt.

"Thank you," I said, ready to move past his explanation. "But we came here to talk about the fairy."

"Yes." He nodded and set his Bible back in the drawer. "I will show you something," he said, stepping over to his desk chair, "and then we will go into the conference room to discuss it. My associate will join us, but no one else. No one else at the station knows about this."

My curiosity was more than piqued. I stepped closer as he sat, then swiveled to the beautiful credenza behind his desk. After taking a key from his pocket, he unlocked a deep drawer in the credenza, then lifted out a glass jar containing clear liquid . . . and a creature that looked identical to the sketch Brenda had drawn on the plane.

I saw her eyes widen, then close tightly. No sense in denying it, I wanted to tell her, when the evidence was right before our eyes.

"*Esta aqui.*" Senior Prospero slid it across the desktop. "*El Hada.* The fairy."

The five of us drew closer. As frightening as Brenda's sketch had been, the creature in the jar was far more terrifying in its gruesome details. The skull was small, but still covered by enough skin that we could see pointed ears and soft fur around the folds. The empty eye sockets were large, and the gaping mouth revealed rows of jagged teeth that reminded me of a shark's. The creature had a visible neck, and a chest covered with what appeared to be black, leathery skin. The skin covered the chest area, two arms, and two legs, both of which ended in hands or feet with five jointed digits each. The creature also had two large wings composed of bone (or cartilage?) and covered with skin.

The thing was incredibly human—far more human than animal. And it was large, for a fairy. About the size of one of my old Barbie dolls.

"Yes," Señor Prospero said, observing our reactions. "It does look like something out of a nightmare. But for the wings, it is humanoid. But you must also see this."

He turned the jar, enabling us to see the oddest feature yet—a tail, long and curving, that ended in a sharp point, almost like a claw or tooth.

"Incredible," Chad whispered.

Tank's response followed: "Jesus, help us."

Brenda said nothing, but kept her arm firmly wrapped around Daniel's shoulders and her gaze on that glass jar.

Chad straightened first. "It has to be a fake," he said, swaying slightly on his feet. "It's a clever fake, but a fake nonetheless."

"How can you know that?" Brenda asked.

Chad shook his head. "These things pop up all the time. Last year two guys in England claimed to find a fairy, and it looked pretty fairy-like. But they released the news on April first, and the thing turned out to be a gigantic April Fool's joke. It was some wire structure with leaves wrapped around it."

Señor Prospero said nothing, but picked up the jar and carried it into the conference room, where he set it in the center of the table. Then he went to a phone, murmured something into it, and sat in the chair at the head of the table, motioning that we should be seated as well.

We had no sooner finished settling into our chairs when another man entered. He wore a white lab coat and glasses.

"I would like to introduce," Señor Prospero said, "Dr. Gregory Wu, an expert in molecular science."

"Great," Brenda whispered under her breath. "We got us a mini-United Nations right here."

When Dr. Wu had seated himself, Prospero leaned forward and clasped his hands on the table. "I own this TV station," he said. "My talk show is live every weekday from one until five. We talk about all kinds of things—politics, religion, economics, and the environment. Many people have encouraged me to run for president, but though I am popular, I am no politician. I am an entertainer. But people see me as more."

He shifted his position, bringing his hand to his face in a gesture I recognized as an anxiety indicator. "Two years ago, a farmer and his twelve-year-old son brought me this—thing." He nodded toward the jar. "They said that since I was on TV, I would know what to do with it. They said they had seen similar things flying at night, but they had never seen a dead specimen. They left it with me, and I put it in this jar of formaldehyde."

He cleared his throat, then gestured to Dr. Wu. "I thought it was a hoax, but wanted to be sure, so I hired Dr. Wu to take X-rays. He did, producing two films—a frontal view and one of the creature in profile." He looked at his associate. "Dr. Wu, would you please distribute the films?"

From a folder, Wu produced two things— actual X-ray films and paper copies of those images. He handed the films to Tank, and the copies to Brenda, indicating that we should pass both around.

For a long while no one said anything. The images were alarming, but the films were obviously genuine. And when viewing the creature straight on, seeing the eye sockets and the mouth open and ringed with teeth—

A ghost spider crawled up my spine as I imagined the fairy alive and moving. What *was* this thing?

"It is one thing," Señor Prospero said, "to cover sticks or wires with leaves and call it a fairy, but what man alive can create a skeleton of bone and cover it with flesh?"

"Hang on," Chad said, slurring his words slightly. "How do you know that's—that's bone?"

"See the calcification at the joints?" Dr. Wu asked. "That is a result of normal wear of bone against bone. And do you see how the calcification is heaviest on the back where the wings join the body? That is what you would expect of a humanoid with wings—the bone is thicker in that area to support the additional weight. That is to be expected, but few would go through such trouble to create a hoax."

Brenda leaned toward me. "Is Chad *drunk*?"

I shook my head. "I think it's his cold medicine. But he does seem a little doped."

"You will also notice," Dr. Wu went on, pointing at a copy of the X-ray, "that the creature has been injured and that injury has been repaired."

I studied my paper copy of the image. I might not have noticed, but Dr. Wu was right—one of the creature's long legs had been broken and the bone clumsily reset. We could see a white spot over the break, as if someone had applied a patch of some sort.

Who would do such a thing? A doctor fairy?

Chad turned the jar to study the creature within. "We could s-settle this question in no time. Have you taken DNA from this—this thing?"

"We have taken samples," Dr. Wu said, "but so far we have been unable to extract DNA because the formaldehyde has destroyed the material. But we have sent samples to other labs in the hope that they can read the DNA sequence."

"That thing is creepy," Brenda said, pushing away from the table as if being near the fairy made her nervous. "It's nasty lookin'."

"It is a *duch*," Daniel said, his wide eyes intent upon the creature.

Señor Prospero frowned. "And what is a duch?"

"We're not sure," I answered, "because sometimes Daniel speaks in his own language. But we do know it's something bad."

"I must admit that Ms. S-Smartmouth makes a good point," Chad said. "If you were going to create a fake creature, you'd want it to look fierce. Just like this."

Brenda cast Chad a killing look, but I pressed on, not wanting the discussion to dissolve into a drug-induced spat.

"Other real animals look terrifying," I argued. "Crocodiles, moray eels, and sharks. They're not fakes."

"Yet people who create hoaxes," Señor Prospero said, "crave and create publicity, but neither the farmer nor his son has ever gone public with this news. I have never mentioned the fairy on my program, nor have I shown it to anyone but my wife and Dr. Wu. But—" he lifted both brows and smiled—"I have been asking God to send me someone who would know what to do with this thing. And here you are."

In that moment I'm not sure who was more dumbfounded—Señor Prospero or our group. Everyone around the table stopped fidgeting as a hush fell over the room.

"We were sent here," I finally said, my voice trembling, "to see this thing, learn about it, and see if we can figure out why it's here."

"It's c-clearly not natural," Chad said, shaking his head. "And I'm not saying it's a fake—I'm saying it's not a natural part of the animal kingdom. I doubt there's anything like it on the planet."

Señor Prospero answered with a sad smile. "Unfortunately, there is." He gestured to Dr. Wu, who pulled out a small box and set a small box on the conference table. When he lifted the lid, we rose from our seats to peer inside. On a soft bed of cotton, we saw the skeleton of another creature, one eerily similar to the first. The skin had desiccated and fallen away, but the skull, the jagged teeth, and the long, slender limbs remained. Along with the wings and the tail.

"You will notice," Dr. Wu said, using his pen to gently probe the remnants of the wings, "this creature has two sets of wings. It was probably—"

"D-deformed?" Chad guessed.

"A prototype," Wu answered. "A first attempt. You will notice that this one is curled up in a fetal position—as if it curled up to die."

I bit my lip. Scientists did not usually make "as

if" statements, but Wu was right—the creature did look as though it had given up.

"Where did you find the second specimen?" I asked.

"A truck driver brought it in," Señor Prospero said. "He struck it with his truck as he was driving one night. When he stopped to see what he had hit, he found it curled up on the truck's fender."

"So . . . you think someone made this," Chad said.

Señor Prospero nodded. "We believe it is a creation, but not a fake. It is a real creature. A hybrid."

I shivered. We had run into hybrids before— the black-eyed children—and the experience had not been pleasant.

Dr. Wu lifted his hand. "This creature is probably 98.5 percent human. As to the remaining 1.5 percent, we can only guess."

"A chimera." Chad smiled. "A blend of two living creatures."

"Exactly." Wu nodded. "The creature could be a chimera composed of human and alien cells. Or human and animal. We will not know its exact makeup until we have an accurate DNA analysis."

"That reminds me," I said. "I just read a newspaper report about this. Apparently the U.S. National Institute of Health is lifting a ban that prevented scientists from creating human-animal chimeras."

Wu shook his head. "The people who are

behind this creature are years ahead of your NIH."

"Does Mexico have a national research program involving chimeras?" I asked.

Señor Prospero shook his head. "Definitely not."

"So whoever is doing this—"

"Is off-book," Prospero said. "Not a national government."

"I have a question," Tank said, lifting the X-ray of the first creature toward the overhead lights. "This creature's skeleton has white dots all through it. What are those?"

Señor Prospero looked at Dr. Wu, then sighed. "We have our theories, but I hesitate to mention them. We are lacking too many facts to be dogmatic."

I looked at Tank and Brenda. "I guess that's where we come in. Our assignment was to verify the creature, try to determine where it came from, and see if we can figure out why it exists."

Prospero smiled. "Not an easy task."

"No," Tank said, meeting the man's gaze. "But we've faced the impossible and survived, so I think we can handle a fairy."

"Hubris," Senor Prospero said, smiling. "You certainly have it in abundance."

"Yes, he does," Chad said, crossing his arms.

Tank beamed . . . I didn't have the heart to tell him the comment wasn't intended to be a compliment.

Chapter 4

With our shiny new credit cards from the Watchers, we rented rooms at a hotel not far from the TV station. Then we met in my suite to lay out a few plans.

"We need to hire a car," I said, unfolding a map I'd picked up in a small store. "We shouldn't be driving around Mexico without knowing where we're going."

"Roger that," Brenda said, and when our eyes met I suspected that she, like me, was thinking about recent news reports. It might have been an unfair characterization, but our local news networks had featured too many stories about

American tourists running into drug lords and ending up with their heads in one location and their bodies in another.

I didn't want to take any chances.

Tank handed me the contact information Señor Prospero had given us when we left. The man who'd brought the fairy to the TV station was Hector Rodriguez, and he lived on a farm about an hour from Mexico City. I had imagined meeting him in a little cafe somewhere, but after looking at the map and seeing nothing but forest, I realized we'd have to go to the man's house.

"Señor Rodriguez lives in the middle of nowhere, apparently," I said, picking up my iPad to check out a satellite view of the area. I tapped on the maps icon, typed in the address, and found myself staring at a narrow road that wound through an area of heavy forest. I zoomed out and saw that our contact lived inside a national park: *Parque Nacional El Tepozteco*. I could see no road leading to his house, but it probably lay beneath the canopy of trees.

"All right." I did a quick computation. "Google maps says we can reach the farmer's house in about an hour, depending on traffic. We'll visit him tomorrow, interview him and his son, and see what they can tell us about the fairy. And while we're in the area, we can look around to see if we can spot anything else."

"We should spend the night," Chad said.

Four other heads swiveled toward him. "Are

you still drunk?" Brenda asked.

"I'm fine." Chad leaned forward, elbows on his knees. "Think about it—this thing flies, and so far it has eluded most people, so I think it's safe to say it's nocturnal. It may even have luminescent qualities, like a firefly. So if it comes out at night, we should stay and look for it. Our bosses told us to get video."

I blew out a breath. "We can't assume that Señor Rodriguez will have room for us—or even want us hanging around."

"We don't have to stay at his house. We find out where he discovered the creature, and we camp there."

Brenda stiffened. "Did you say *camp*?"

Chad grinned. "Haven't you ever spent the night out under the stars?"

"Not by choice."

"It's easy. We just need to rent a tent, some sleeping bags, and some canteens. We can all share the tent, and Andi and I will double up with a sleeping bag."

"Whoa," I said, my face flushing hot against the air conditioned air. "This is not the time for joking around—and those kinds of jokes aren't welcome here, not now or ever."

Chad lifted his hands in a posture of surrender. "Cool your jets, sweetie. I was only testing the waters."

"Well, stop it." I bit my lip, frustrated that I couldn't think of witty remarks as quickly as a doped-up Chad. "Or I'll . . . you'll regret it."

Chad grinned. He was probably reading my mind, hearing me regret my inability to think on my feet . . .

"Or," Brenda went on, ignoring Chad, "we could pick up some snacks, bottled water, and have someone make us a gourmet picnic basket. There's no law saying we have to rough it out there."

"You guys discuss it," I told them, standing. "I'll be back in a minute."

I left them in the living room and went to the restroom. After washing my hands, I stared in the mirror for a long moment and tried to imagine what I'd look like after a night out in the Mexican woods. Mexico was in the tropics, which meant lots of humidity. It also meant spiders and snakes grew even bigger down here, and maybe more venomous. Not to mention the mosquitoes. We'd not only need a tent, we'd need mosquito repellent, fly swatters, rain ponchos, a couple of lanterns, something to start a fire, and maybe a portable toilet . . .

I laughed and imagined my hair as a big red dish scrubber. Maybe I should get a hat. I'd never been camping in my life, but I was up for anything, as long as everyone else came along.

I dried my hands on a towel, then glanced in the mirror to make sure my hair hadn't gone completely out of control in the humidity. Then I stopped cold.

The professor was in my mirror. He smiled when our eyes met, and my heart did a strange little flipflop. Was I seeing things? Did I miss him so much that I was imagining him in my mirror?

I closed my eyes and counted—one, two, three. I lifted my eyelids and saw him standing there, arms crossed, that funny little smile below his mustache. He was humoring me.

"Where are you?" I asked.

He tapped his left wrist—shorthand for referring to time--then he pointed—not *at* me, but *beyond* me—and the gesture lifted the hairs on my arms. Could he always see us from where he was? If he was in a parallel universe, did his have gruesome fairies, too? I opened my mouth, about to say something else, but before I could speak he vanished. Gone. Just like that.

I exhaled in sharp disappointment. My former boss and good friend had been *right there* . . . unless my brain had conjured him up. Chad would say that I wanted his advice, so my subconscious had provided him, neat and tidy and pointing at me as if to say *You can do it, Andi.*

Except he hadn't been exactly pointing at me. He'd been pointing beyond me, at something in the bedroom.

I turned. And saw a folder on the bed. A striking silver folder with my name on the cover. A folder I had never seen in my life.

As every nerve in my body screamed *impossible*, I walked over and picked it up. And inside I found a biography of Ambrosi Giacomo, a man I'd never heard of.

Moving slowly on legs that felt like wood, I went back to the living room. "Guys," I said, interrupting their conversations. I held up the silver folder. "Anyone ever seen this before?"

They stared at it.

"Where'd you get that?" Brenda asked. "Party City?"

"Never seen it," Tank said, speaking for everyone. His eyes softened with concern. "You okay? You look a little rattled."

I set the folder on the coffee table, then sank back into my chair. "I went into the bathroom and nothing was on the bed. And as I was washing my hands, I saw the professor in the mirror. He pointed behind me, and just as I was about to say something to him, he disappeared. When I turned around, this was on the bed."

Chad brightened. "Cool."

Brenda looked at him as if he'd sprung a brain leak. "Are you insane? This sort of thing doesn't happen . . . much."

"I've seen the professor in mirrors before," I reminded them. "But afterward I've never found anything . . . tangible."

"It's real," Daniel said, smiling. "It's from him."

"I suppose," Chad said, "if your professor traveled to a different dimension via a fold in the space-time continuum, he might have found a way to transport certain materials. Like a folder."

"Never seen one like that," Brenda said. "What's it made of, plastic?"

I ran my fingertips over the folder. "Not plastic. Not paper. Something else."

Tank slapped his blue-jeaned thighs. "Who cares what it's made of? What's in it?"

I opened the folder again, relieved to discover that the contents hadn't changed or disappeared. "It's a bio of some man I've never heard of— Ambrosi Giacomo. Does that name ring a bell with anyone?"

I looked around the circle—Chad, Tank, Brenda, Daniel—nothing.

But Brenda whipped out her phone. "We don't have to stay ignorant." She typed on the keyboard, then nodded. "There's a Wikipedia entry—not a long one, but enough to prove the man exists. In our world, that is."

"And?" Chad prodded.

"Chillax, man, I'm readin'." She skimmed the material, then looked up. "He's some kind of businessman in Italy. Rich, apparently. And that's all it says."

"A photo?" I asked, wondering if Ambrose Giacomo and Benedicto Prospero could be the same person.

Brenda shook her head. "No picture. Says he was born in 1983. In Italy."

I looked at Tank. "Ambrose Giacomo is not another name for Benedicto Prospero. The Italian guy is too young."

"Does the article mention his companies?" Chad asked. "His line of work?"

"No and no." Brenda dropped her phone back into her purse. "Sorry."

"Maybe it's a false name," Chad said. "Or maybe the Italian dude is the Mexican dude's son."

"Maybe this stuff has nothing to do with the fairy," Brenda said. "If the professor is off in another world, how do we know his world matches up with ours? Maybe he's screwed up. Or maybe the worlds are similar, but Señor Prospero is Ambrose Giacomo in the professor's world—and he's younger."

"Or—" Chad lifted a finger—"Maybe the professor is warning us about something in the future. Maybe this Ambrose Giacomo is a kind of Hitler in the professor's world, so he's warning us. Or maybe he just wants us to keep an eye on the guy."

"Maybe the countries are different," Tank said. "Maybe Italy is Mexico in the professor's world and Mexico is something else. Maybe Ambrose whoever is investigating the fairies in the professor's world—"

"Enough." I dropped my head into my hands. "You're giving me a headache."

We sat for a moment in silence, then Chad stood and stretched. "You gals can stay here and rest up if you want, but the big lug and I should

ANGELA HUNT

go out and get some camping equipment. Andi, be a sweetheart and reserve our car. Do we want to leave this afternoon or tomorrow?"

I bristled at his be a sweetheart comment, but decided to ignore it . . . because he was still under the influence.

"Tomorrow," I said, looking at Brenda to see if she agreed. "I think we need to do a little more planning."

"And we're chargin' batteries," Brenda added. "We're chargin' our phones, our iPads, the camera, the bug zappers, and anything else you guys buy. I'm not headin' into the woods without a full supply of energized gadgets."

"Good idea," I said. "So you guys go shopping and I'll reserve a car for tomorrow morning."

Ready or not, fairies and goblins, we were on our way.

Chapter 5

By the time our hired car arrived at the hotel the next morning, we looked like a group of city slickers heading out for an overpriced wilderness adventure. Chad and Tank had gone a little overboard collecting supplies. They not only bought a tent, they also purchased cots, mosquito netting, butterfly nets (the perfect thing for catching fairies, Tank said), a Coleman stove, three Coleman lanterns, rain ponchos, a tarp, a folding table (with seats, Chad pointed out), a portable toilet, a bug zapper, toilet paper, a privacy screen, a six pack of flashlights, five sleeping bags, a cooler, and enough water, soft drinks, and groceries to supply us for a week.

Naturally, half of what they brought wouldn't fit into the rented vehicle.

The driver stood outside the hotel shaking his head. "*Esta materia no cabrá.*"

"We can make it work," Chad said. "It's all a matter of design. If we arrange the items geometrically—"

"Not gonna work," Tank said. "You have to shove the stuff in. If we push it all in the back, it'll fit."

I stood in the driveway and looked at the load, then at the space in the large SUV. Add in five passengers, our luggage and personal belongings—

"It won't work," I said firmly. "So here's what you're going to leave behind. The portable table—"

"But—" Chad protested.

"It's too big, and we can sit in the tent. Leave out the toilet and the privacy screen."

Brenda snorted. "You planning on holding it for twenty-four hours?"

"A tree will work fine, and the toilet paper goes with us. But not the giant pack. Two or three rolls, tops."

Chad grinned. "I love it when she plays wilderness woman."

I ignored him. He seemed sharp again, but his eyes were a bit watery and I'd already heard him sneeze three times.

"We take enough food for two meals—and water for two days," I said. "No more. We don't need the stove. We only need one lantern. If we keep the tent zipped, we won't need mosquito netting. You can bring one butterfly net. Ditch the cots, we can sleep on the ground. If there's room, you can bring the sleeping bags, but make sure they're rolled tightly."

Tank peered at me, his eyes narrow. "Were you a Girl Scout?"

"I'm practical. Anyone can see that you guys bought too much."

Thirty minutes later, we had packed the car and pulled away from the hotel, leaving a neat pile of camping gear beneath a sign that read: *¡Gratis! Si te gusta acampar.*

* * *

An hour later, I straightened in the front passenger seat and showed my phone and its map app to the driver. "We're close," I said, trying to remember the Spanish words. "*Estamos cerca. Maneja lento.*"

He gave me an uncertain look, but slowed the car so we could search for signs along the road. We had driven about ten miles into the national park when the app indicated that we had reached our destination. Frantic, I looked out the window and spotted a barely visible dirt road snaking through the trees. "*¡Aqui!* I mean, *Por ahí!*"

The driver turned. As the SUV rumbled over

the road, jostling our equipment and rattling our teeth, the driver muttered Spanish expletives under his breath. Finally we pulled up in front of a modest house surrounded by several outbuildings. A skinny dog ran over to the car, barking as if there were no tomorrow, but the animal shied away when I opened my door.

"We don't want to scare this farmer," I said, realizing that the sight of a big, black SUV might alarm anyone. "So let me go speak to him. The rest of you can get out and stretch your legs, but don't snoop. And don't wander off."

"Why don't you let me go talk to him?" Chad said, unbuckling his seat belt. "After all, I can read his mind. I could—"

He sneezed so explosively that Brenda's dreads swayed in the resulting breeze.

"Thought you couldn't read a mind that thought in Spanish," Brenda said.

"Yeah, but I can still sense things. Fear. Deception. Irritation."

"You're staying in the car," I told him, feeling irritated myself. "I speak more Spanish than you do, and I'm a woman. Women are less threatening."

"But—"

"No buts, newbie. I can handle this. And by the way—" I exhaled in resignation. "Take another one of those antihistamines. We'll never see a fairy if you scare them off with all that sneezing."

Chad tossed me a mock salute. "Yes, ma'am."

I blew out a breath. I had felt a certain amount of tension between us over the past few days—almost as if Chad expected to be anointed team leader and thought I was usurping his position. But our team didn't actually *have* a leader, so he shouldn't be getting his nose out of joint if I did my best to keep things organized.

I got out and slowly approached the house. The farm might be considered poor by American standards, but it looked pretty prosperous to me. A large water tank sat on the flat roof, and someone had painted the stucco exterior bright blue with coral accents on the door and windowsills. A chicken coop sat behind the house, and a couple of other buildings stood beyond the henhouse. In the distance, a couple of acres had been planted with something that grew lush and green in the hot sun.

"¡*Hola*!" I called. "¿*Alguien en casa*?"

A moment later a man appeared behind the screen door. He wore dark pants and a sleeveless undershirt, and he regarded me with a wary gaze. Behind him, just over his shoulder, I saw a young teenager, probably thirteen or fourteen.

"Hola!" I smiled and waved in an effort to appear friendly. "¿*Hablan ustedes Inglés*?"

The father looked at me, then gestured to the kid, who stepped out from behind him. "My father doesn't speak English," the boy said, "but I can translate."

"Good." I smiled in relief. "My name is Andi, and my friends and I are from the United States. Yesterday we spoke to Señor Prospero from the TV station. He gave us your address."

The boy nodded. "Si."

"We'd like to talk to you about the creature you found. And we'd like to see the place—where you found him, that is."

The boy looked at his father and explained in a flood of Spanish. The older man scratched his chin, then looked at me and responded. I didn't catch a word.

"My father," the kid said, "wants me to tell you I found it lying in a ditch. I was riding my bicycle and stopped—" he looked down—"to make water, and that's when I saw it."

I nodded, slowly understanding. So the kid stopped to obey the call of nature. Happens to everyone.

"Was the creature dead when you found it?"

"Si—yes."

"Had you ever seen anything like that before?"

The boy glanced at his father, who nodded.

"Si. Sometimes at night, we see them flying. Once we saw one come out of a tree."

I blinked. "It was in the tree? Up in the branches?"

The boy shook his head. "It was—*¿como dice que?*—it came out of a hole in the tree."

"Ah." I considered his answer, then asked, "Why did you take the creature to Señor

Prospero?"

The kid looked at his father, repeated the question in Spanish, and listened to his father's reply.

"Papa said Señor Prospero always takes questions from the audience and gets answers. But we have not had an answer yet. Señor Prospero has not even talked about the creature."

"Not yet." I glanced back at the others, who appeared to be waiting patiently. "I'm sorry, I forgot to ask your name."

The boy gave me a shy smile. "Tomas."

"Tomas, could you take us to the place where you found the fairy? We would like to spend the night in that spot so we can help Señor Prospero find some answers."

The boy's eyes widened, then he translated for his father. The elder Rodriguez eyed me for a long moment, then nodded and pointed to a bicycle propped against a tree.

"Papa says I am to lead you there and then come home," Tomas said. "I will be ready in a minute."

"Take your time," I said, grateful that the family wanted to cooperate. "We'll follow you."

The boy disappeared into the house, leaving me with Señor Rodriguez. I smiled, then remembered my manners. "Gracias, señor. Muchas gracias."

He nodded, then went back into the house, leaving me to wait for his son.

* * *

"So Tomas is going to take us to the spot," I told the others, "and we can set up camp there."

"This is a national park," Tank pointed out. "Aren't there rules against camping in a national park?"

"You're confused," Chad said, his voice sharp and cynical. "Everybody camps in the national parks. The rules prohibit littering."

I looked at Brenda, who shrugged. "It's not like we're plannin' to live there," she pointed out. "We'll actually only be there a few hours, and we'll clean up. Nonexistent footprint and all that."

"Right." I sighed. "As long as we don't get arrested."

Being jailed in Mexico wasn't my idea of fun, but we hadn't seen any signs that prohibited camping. In fact, since entering the Parque Nacional El Tepozteco, we hadn't seen any signs or any forest rangers. In any case, the Rodriguez family lived within the park boundaries, so how strict could the rules be?

A few moments later Tomas appeared, wearing a button-up shirt, jeans, and sneakers. He picked up his bike and smiled. "Ready?"

"Lead the way, Tomas." I hopped back in the car along with the others. The driver did a three-point turn and we followed Tomas back to the paved two-lane road.

We drove a couple of miles down the

serpentine highway, then Thomas turned onto another dirt road, this one much less-traveled that the one that led to his house. Our driver complained again, but he kept driving, moving slowly over the ruts and maneuvering around fallen trees and branches. Finally the shrubbery and trees at the side of the road opened up to reveal a ditch running along a barren field. The boy stopped and swung his leg over his bike.

Our driver braked to a halt.

"*Aquí.*" Tomas pointed to the ditch. "The fairy was in the ditch."

We piled out of our vehicle. The ditch was nothing extraordinary—only a foot deep, with weeds growing on the banks and a trickle of muddy brown water at the bottom. The field beyond had probably been planted at some point, but now resembled nothing except dry, brown earth. Trees to the right and left provided a curtain of shade for the rutted road, effectively concealing it from overhead planes or helicopters or Google Earth cameras.

Chad stepped closer. "Has it occurred to you—" he scratched his chin—"that this might be the perfect place to grow wacky tabacky?"

"What?"

"Marijuana." He lowered his voice. "Secluded spot, mostly covered from above, no traffic or prying eyes—"

"We're not the DEA," I told him. "We're here to investigate a scientific anomaly."

"But maybe we should consider an illegal drug operation as a reason for the creature," he said, whispering out of the side of his mouth. "Maybe the family made up the story to scare people away from this part of the forest. Maybe some drug lord paid big bucks for a sophisticated fake fairy, and this is all a cover-up—"

"If they wanted to scare people away, they've done a poor job of it," I reminded him. "Did you check the Internet? I did. There was a plastic Tinkerbell that folks in some small Mexican village are charging people to view, and another fake in an unspecified location. But there's been nothing about *this* story. That's *nada* in Spanish."

Chad grinned. "You are *so* cute when you're ticked off. How do you manage it?"

I curled my hands into fists until the urge to slap him had passed.

Moving toward Tomas, I pulled out my phone and showed him a copy of the creature's X-ray. "Does this look like the creature you gave Señor Prospero?"

The boy's eyes widened. "*Si. Claro.* But . . . it looks different."

"This is an X-ray," I said. "The thick parts look white, and the thinner parts are darker." I pointed to one of the strange white spots on the creature's body. "Do you have any idea what those white spots could be?"

He looked closer, then his eyes widened and his expression twisted. He glanced away, then bit his lip and looked at me, guilt written all over his face.

"Tomas—do you know what those spots are?"

He kept his mouth clamped shut as he looked from left to right.

"Tomas, if you help us, we may be able to find answers. Your father would like an answer, right?"

The boy nodded.

"So if you know anything at all—"

"He shot it." The words tripped off his tongue. "The night before I found it, we were outside and we saw them. They came close to the house, and we saw the face. Mama screamed, so Papa got his *escopeta* and shot it."

A dozen thoughts tumbled through my mind. If Señor Rodriguez shot the creature, it should have been blasted to smithereens. But perhaps that depended on what an *escopeta* was.

"Tomas—*¿que es una escopeta?*"

He squinched up his face, then lifted an imaginary gun—or maybe a crossbow—to his face and shoulder, then pulled the trigger.

So . . . rifle? Bow? I didn't know much about weapons.

I walked over to speak to our driver. "*Escopeta, por favor,*" I asked. "*¿Que is escopeta?*"

He gave me a blank look, then pulled a language dictionary from his pocket. After a moment, he looked up. "Shotgun."

I looked at Tank, who had followed me over.

"Buckshot." His smile broadened into a grin. "And, by golly, if those dots aren't the perfect size for buckshot. The thing must have been too quick to get the full blast, but it still got hit by six or seven pellets."

I heard an almost-audible click as the pieces of the puzzle fell into place.

"This is the spot," I told the driver. "We're going to unload here. If you could pick us up here at this time tomorrow, we'll pay double the charge and give you the extra as a gratuity."

In that moment, the man had no problem understanding my English. He hopped out of the car and opened the back hatch. "Okay," he said, grabbing the closest suitcase. "Okey-dokey."

Chapter 6

An hour later the five of us sat around a pile of logs that was supposed to be a campfire. I couldn't believe it, but though we had purchased everything we could think of to camp successfully, we hadn't bothered to learn how to light a fire.

"A bunch of stupid city slickers, that's what we are," Brenda said, slapping at a bug buzzing her ankles. "Nobody ever told me I'd need to know how to start a fire."

"I can't believe we didn't bring matches," Chad complained for the fourth time. "I assumed one of you ladies would carry them in your purse."

"Nobody smokes anymore," I said. "Lung cancer isn't glamorous."

Chad looked at Tank. "Didn't you learn how to rub two sticks together back there in Podunkville where you grew up?"

Tank glared back. "I haven't seen you creating any sparks. I've seen you *tryin'* to get somethin' goin', but it ain't gonna happen—"

"Guys!" I shouted, aware that they weren't talking about the fire any more.

Sighing, I crossed my legs and looked toward the western horizon, where the sun was about to disappear behind a wall of trees. "Maybe we don't need a fire. We still have a lantern, right?"

Chad grinned. "Yeah . . . and it has ignomatic autonition." He laughed. "I mean automatic ignition."

"His medicine just kicked in," Brenda said, shaking her head.

He opened a box, pulled out the lantern and struggled to read the instructions in the fading light. Fortunately, the lantern blazed into light just as the sun disappeared and the sky turned from blue to blue-black.

"Ouch!" Brenda slapped at her bare arm, then looked at the tent. "Maybe we should get inside before the kamikaze mosquitos come out. I don't want Daniel gettin' a thousand bites."

"Sounds good to me." I picked up my stuff

and moved inside the tent, where earlier Brenda and Daniel had rolled out five sleeping bags and covered nearly all the floor. The tent had several windows, and the guys had rolled up the canvas coverings so we could keep watch from behind the screens.

"Come on, Daniel," Brenda said, practically lifting him from the spot where he'd been playing his hand-held video game. "You're about to wear out the batteries on that thing."

"Yowie!" Tank slapped at his arm, then Chad hit his neck. "Man! Let's get inside!"

The guys followed us into the tent. As Tank zipped up the entrance and Chad powered on the bug zapper, Brenda and I sat before one of the front windows, watching for anything unusual in the air, the trees, or the weeds.

"These things glow, right?" Tank said.

"I'm not sure," I answered. "Dr. Wu didn't say anything about glowing. Neither did Tomas."

"How are we supposed to see 'em if they don't glow?"

"Look for the light," I told him. "The moon is supposed to be full tonight."

"Romantic," Chad said. "I wuv it."

"Not the time or place for such talk," I said, scowling at Chad. "Besides, you're manning the video camera, right?"

"Yep." He patted the pouch hanging from his belt. "I got it covered."

I felt the air move, then heard Tank hit the

canvas floor next to me. "Thought I'd sit here to guard the door," he said, moving so close that his arm brushed mine. "Wouldn't want a bear or anything to come after our food."

"I don't think a bear is going to crash the place for a box of protein bars," Brenda said, her voice as dry as the aforementioned bars. "And that reminds me—Chad, toss me one of those water bottles, will ya?"

I heard the crinkle of plastic behind me, then silence reigned as we settled into position and waited.

"You know," Chad said after a few minutes, "Tank, maybe I should sit in the doorway. I've got the video camera, after all, and that's the biggest opening. I might need all that space to get the shot."

Tank thrust his arm toward Chad. "Hand it over. I can work the camera."

Chad patted the lump on his belt. "No need, I studied the manual. This is going to require a low light setting, and it takes a bit of expertise to get a useable image."

"So set the settings for me," Tank insisted. "Just hand me the camera."

"Naw—let me sit there to tape."

"The taping isn't as important as protection. What if someone or something comes through? Do you think your hundred and thirty pounds could stop a bear?"

"One hundred seventy," Chad said, a thread of

indignation in his voice. "And I don't think there are any bears in Mexico."

"How do you know there aren't?"

"How do you know there *are*?"

"Good grief." Exasperated beyond belief, I got up and moved to the far side of the tent, where I could sit by Daniel. He was paying more attention to his video game than his surroundings.

Brenda snorted.

Chad sank to the canvas, and he and Tank finally stopped bickering.

Time stretched itself thin as we watched and waited. A steady churring of insects rose from the weeds, rising in unison crescendos and diminuendos as if commanded by some invisible director. A sough of wind rustled the branches of the pines around us, sending pine needles spinning to earth. The full moon rose, silvering the landscape and allowing us to see without being seen. Ideal conditions, really. Almost as if our bosses had arranged this, too.

"Look at that." Tank pointed toward the spot where we had been trying to light a fire. Something fluttered there, and once it struck the earth, we heard a high squeal and the soft flap of wings.

"Owl catching mouse," Chad said. "Not fairy."

Tank nodded. "Right."

"That squeak?" Chad laughed. "Reminds me of . . . when I was a kid and my dad . . . used to look at me."

Brenda turned her head. "Who squeaked, you or him?"

He released a hollow laugh. "You'd have squeaked, too, if you'd had William Jack Thorton as your daddy."

The statement hung in the air, inviting questions.

All right, then. "Was your father stern?" I asked.

Chad exhaled in a rush. "Think of the worst father . . . you've ever seen on TV or in a movie, then multiply by two. That was my dad."

"Oh." I sent a sympathetic smile through the gloom. "I'm really sorry."

"'Sokay," Chad said, locking his hands around his bent knees as he stared out the window. The moonlight painted his face with the colors of iron and steel. "I suppose I wouldn't be the stud I am if I . . . hadn't had a terrible childhood. I learned to draw inside myself . . . whenever things got rough, and that's how I . . . discovered my g-gift. I learned that I could leave and g-go places, you know?"

"I'm still sorry you had to suffer like that," I told him. "No kid should survive childhood by the skin of their teeth. But I'm glad you survived."

I studied Chad, wondering if he wanted to keep talking or let the matter rest. Though I suspected he wouldn't have said any of those things if the medicine hadn't made him dopey and emotional, his chin quivered, so I looked away. I had never met a man—sober or under the influence—who wanted to weep in front of friends, so time to keep quiet for a while.

Zzzzt! At least the battery-powered bug zapper was working.

Time crawled by. I checked my phone and learned that what felt like a couple of hours was only forty minutes. I sighed, realizing that the best thing about sleep was that it made the nighttime hours pass quickly.

I was beginning to wish I had packed my earphones when I saw movement in the moonlight. I squinted through the screen mesh, then rose to my knees and moved closer. Two figures fluttered around the trunk of a pine tree, around and up, in and out in random movements.

"Psst." I looked across the tent, where Brenda and Tank were heavy-lidded and fighting sleep. "Two figures, by that half-dead pine. Whaddya think?"

Tank rose to his knees and knelt behind the entrance screen as if daring the moonlight dancers to do us harm. Chad nudged Brenda and pointed to the creatures, then he moved closer to the window as well. Daniel put down his video game and stood, pressing his hands to the screen as he watched, mesmerized.

The dancing figures came closer. Composed of light and shadow, they circled a bush, teased a flower bud, and hovered over the logs of our unlit fire. Like hands on a clock they moved together, perfectly synchronized, a dance of practiced partners. Then one of them broke away and fluttered toward our tent.

Silence sifted over us, a silence of suspended breathing. We could see it now—this was no bat, no bird, but a creature with a human-like head, arms, legs, and torso. The fairy hovered about four feet from the door, and even from where I sat I could see details on the body—arms, legs, fingers, toes. The head with its downy pointed ears. The lips, closed now, hiding those jagged teeth. And the wings, fanning so quickly they were barely visible.

The creature tilted its head and regarded us, then flew across the front of the tent, peering in at us even as we stared out at—him? Her? Did female fairies wear little dresses made of flower petals?

"Okay," Tank said, and before I could ask what he had in mind, I heard the metallic slide of the zipper. Tank leapt out, the butterfly net in his hand. He sprang forward, the net dipping and swooping and *missing*. The fairy did not flee, but floated up, out of range. Tank took another swipe, and another, but the fairy taunted him, dancing above his flailing arms.

"Tank, will you *m-move*?"

Chad stood outside, the video camera in his hand, his gaze intent on the small screen resting against his palm. He was trying to focus on the fairy, but the thing was elusive and fast, always remaining out of the frame, out of focus—

A bloodcurdling scream shattered the stillness. I turned, horrified by the sound, and saw Daniel arching his back, his mouth open in a paroxysm of terror, his eyes so wide they seemed about to fall out of his face. Somehow, the second fairy had entered the tent and was riding the collar of Daniel's shirt. Not until I moved behind Daniel could I see that the fairy's tail had embedded itself in his clothing, perhaps even into the boy's flesh, because the kid was screaming as if someone had knifed him—

"Get. Away. From. My. Son!"

Brenda picked up the lantern and swung it at the fairy's head, putting everything she had into the blow. The bottom edge of the lantern caught the fairy's chin, knocking it backward, but it remained attached to Daniel's upper back, the tail firmly embedded in his shirt. Not knowing what else to do, I grabbed the creature around the middle, squeezing as I pulled it away from our boy. Something stabbed at my thumb, and I looked down in time to see the creature's teeth at my skin, gnawing my flesh while I tried to pull it away from Daniel—

Brenda approached again, this time with an iPad in one hand and her flashlight in the other. Holding the iPad as a backboard, she slammed the head of the flashlight into the fairy's skull, smashing it and sending a trail of black ooze over my hand and the tablet's shattered screen.

I looked down at the canvas floor where Daniel lay on his tummy, a dark black stain marbling the back of his shirt.

"Is that—is that from that thing?" Brenda asked, her voice trembling. "Or—"

"Help me move him; I can't see."

Together we pulled/dragged an unconscious Daniel into the moonlight, then we pulled up the back of his shirt. I had yanked the fairy away, but the stinger remained—I could see it shining like a polished claw amid a puddle of blood. I tried grasping it with my fingers, but my fingers were slippery and the stinger too firmly embedded—in what? Daniel's skin? His muscle?

Horror snaked down my backbone as I looked up and saw the same emotion reflected in Tank's and Chad's faces. And Brenda—

"My boy." She knelt beside him, terrified to move him, yet aching to draw him into her arms. "What are we gonna do? Andi, we need help, we gotta help him—"

"We're gonna get help." I reached for my phone and pounded 911. Nothing.

"Quick." I looked at Chad. "What's the emergency number for Mexico?"

He looked like a man who had just been told he was dying. "Why s-should I know *that*?"

"It's 66," Brenda said, wringing her hands. "I looked it up before we left—just in case."

I pressed six-six and waited. Nothing.

I stood and moved around, watching the bars on my phone. "I can't get a signal," I said, my panic increasing. "Tank, Chad—you guys got anything?"

As they pulled out their phones to check, I kept pounding the six and waiting for some response. "I had a signal at the Rodriguez house," I said. "How could there be no signal here? We're not that far away."

"We could be in a valley," Chad said, exasperatingly logical, even now. "Or the signal could be blocked by a mountain."

Leaping up, Brenda was on me before I had time to react. "Andi," she said, her fingers gathering up the fabric at the neckline of my shirt. "My boy needs help. I don't know how you're going to get it, but I know you are. Because you always come through. You see things the rest of us miss, so if you ever saw anything, I need you to see a way to help my boy. Now. Right now."

I stared into the whites of her eyes and felt her breath on my face. "Okay," I whispered, placing my hands over hers. "Go—go sit with Daniel. Watch over him."

She obeyed, and I looked up at Tank, who had been watching the treeline for the fairy that got away. "Your gift," I said simply. "Can you help him?"

Tank tilted his head, but immediately sank into the soft earth where Daniel lay. He closed his eyes for what seemed like moments woven of eternity, then he laid his hands on the boy.

We waited. Brenda kept feeling Daniel's forehead and watching the wound on his back as if she expected the stinger to float out and disappear. But nothing happened.

"He's hotter than ever," she said, her voice breaking as she looked up at Tank. "Please." Tears streamed over her cheeks. "Cowboy, you gotta do something for him."

"I'm goin' to."

He looked at me, and in that instant I knew he meant to run. "Okay," I said. "Take Chad—no, Chad needs to stay with Brenda. You and I are going to run to the Rodriguez place and wake them up. We're going to get an ambulance out here."

"Wait." Chad held up his arm, blocking Tank. "You don't need to run. All I hafta do is—you know, go into a trance. I can find someone around here and tell them to get us an ambulance. I'll send firefighters—"

"Medics," I said, grabbing his shirt. "It's not a fire, it's a medical emergency."

Chad waved my hand away. "I can do it. I've done stuff like this my whole life, so I can handle it. You just hafta let me sit here—"

He pointed to the ground, then stumbled forward and fell. "Ya see? I'll go into a trance and find someone. Just watch. You and Tank—you two don't hafta go anywhere alone. That wouldn't be good, no sir. Just sit here where I can keep an eye on ya, and wait while I save the day."

He closed his eyes then and I shifted my gaze to Tank. "He's lost it."

"Leave him," Tank whispered. "Let him see if he can do something while we run to the farm."

"He can't help us," I answered. "He doesn't speak English; his brain is practically out of order—"

"Don't feel sorry for him, Andi," Tank said, his voice surprisingly firm. "We don't have the time."

He pulled his flashlight from his back pocket and shone the light on the road. "Brenda, be careful," he said. "We know there's still one fairy out there somewhere, but there may be others. Okay?"

Brenda nodded, but she didn't seem to be thinking about the threat to herself or Chad. She was focused on Daniel.

"Okay," Tank said, taking my arm. "Let's go."

I paused only long enough to squeeze Brenda's shoulder. "Your boy is going to be okay."

She answered with a heartrending sob.

Chapter 7

Tank and I jogged about twenty yards before we stopped. "Ya know," Tank said, "we are wastin' a lot of time running south, then west, and then north. Wouldn't it be faster if we just cut through the woods and ran west?"

"But running through the woods—that could be risky. We can't see much in the dark, there could be water or bogs to slog through, or we might run into wild animals or even cliffs—"

"I'm just trying to be smart, Andi."

"I know." I looked into his eyes, so soft and concerned. "But it's still risky."

"I would never want to leave you," he said.

"But if we split up here, one of us might be able to reach the farm faster . . . and every second might count for my little buddy."

I understood his reasoning. Tank was an athlete, a faster and stronger runner than I was. Even going through the woods, he was likely to reach the Rodriguez house before me, because I was not an athlete. In college, I took bowling and archery for physical education because I wouldn't have to run anywhere.

"You'll be safe on the road," he said. "I doubt you'll see any cars at this hour, but be careful anyway. I'm going to take off through the woods."

"Just—" My words died away. I was about to tell him to be careful, but this wasn't the time to be overly cautious. Daniel's life was hanging in the balance, so this wasn't a time to take care, but to take risks.

Somehow I managed a rueful smile. "Sure wish we had those comm units. I'd feel better hearing your voice in my ear."

"Roger that." He grinned. "Okay—I'll meet you at the farm. See ya soon."

I waited, taking a moment to catch my breath as I watched him disappear into the brush. I stood on the dirt road and listened until I could no longer hear twigs snapping and branches rustling, then I took off toward the highway, walking as fast as I could.

I had gone maybe a quarter of a mile when I

saw something that halted me in my steps. Several of the creatures were fluttering in a group just off the road ahead. Knowing that they were anything but harmless, I moved to the other side of the road and kept moving. But when my shoe kicked a pebble, the creatures scattered into the woods.

Curious, I walked to the spot where they had congregated. I thought the fairies had been flying around a hole in a fallen tree, but no tree lay on the ground at that spot. Instead, behind a bush I saw a tall rock with a vertical cleft in it—I suppose *fissure* would be a better word. I wanted to find a stick and probe the opening to see if the creatures had come from a cave, but I couldn't take the time to explore.

I kept walking. The distance from the highway to the campsite had felt short when we were in the car, but on foot, the distance seemed like miles. I walked until a felt a stitch in my side, then I drew deep breaths and tried jogging. When I was certain I couldn't take another step, I bent over, held my knees, and took deep breaths while thinking about Daniel and Brenda. I had to keep going for them.

Finally, I reached the highway. Pavement! I would have done a little happy dance, but I had to keep going. I swung my arms like a power walker and kept going.

I nearly missed the dirt road that led to the Rodriguez house, but I got my second wind when I turned down their driveway and headed for the house. When I saw the blue house glowing in the moonlight, I looked around for Tank—either I had beaten him, or he had already called an ambulance and was inside the house.

But no lights burned in the house. I pounded on the door, knowing that Tank hadn't yet arrived. He would have been outside waiting for me.

No one answered, so I pounded the door again. When a light bloomed in the window and the door opened a crack, I explained as quickly as I could: "Señor Rodriguez, it's me, Andi, and we have a medical emergency. Can you please call an ambulance? *Medico*? Our little boy is hurt."

The door opened, and in the lamplight I saw Señor Rodriguez in a tee shirt and boxer shorts, his shotgun in his hand. He nodded and opened the door, and in the background I saw his wife on the phone, already calling for help.

I collapsed in a chair and wiped sweat from my dripping forehead. I closed my eyes for a moment to catch my breath, and when I looked up, Tomas sat on the couch in front of me. "Are you okay?" he asked.

I nodded. "But Daniel—the little boy with us—he was stung. He's very sick."

Tomas shook his head and pointed to my hand. I turned and gasped when I saw that my right hand was caked in blood, the side of my thumb raw and ravaged from where the creature had exercised its incisors. "Ouch," I said, feeling suddenly woozy. "I guess I could use a Band-Aid, if you have one."

Tomas said something to his mother, then Señora Rodriguez came toward me, pulling the edges of her housecoat together as she exclaimed over my wound. She made motherly clucking sounds, then left and returned a few moments later with a bowl of water and bandages.

As she murmured soothing words and bandaged my thumb, I smiled, whispered "gracias" and tried to be attentive . . . while my thoughts centered on Daniel and Tank, who was still out in the woods fighting only-God-knew-what.

Chapter 8

It must have been a slow night in Coajomulco, the town nearest the Rodriguez farm, because they sent two ambulances in response to our call. Señor Rodriguez rode with the first one and went to pick up Daniel, but I urged the second to wait for Tank, who had not yet appeared at the farm. I told Tomas about Tank, and he kept trying to tell the medics that we needed help to find Tank. I wasn't exactly sure what the medics were saying, but the gist seemed to be that they weren't searchers, they were medical personnel. "But if

Tank is in the woods," I reminded Tomas, "he might have been attacked by the same creatures that attacked Daniel."

Tomas tried again to explain that we might need medical assistance, but with no success.

As the second ambulance pulled away, I went outside and sat on a tree stump, surprised to find the sky brightening in the east. Sunrise. Blue skies and the touch of reality. A world where dark fairies did not watch through your windows.

I lifted my gaze to that blue-pink sky and found myself yearning for Tank's God. I knew Him too, of course, as HaShem, but Tank seemed to be on a first-name basis with the Deity, while I had always remained at arms' length.

"Master of the Universe," I began—

A huge bush rustled at my left and I tensed, afraid one of the creatures had come back for a last-minute lashing. But then the branches parted and Tank appeared—muddy, rumbled, bleeding, but most definitely alive.

"Tank!" I leapt up and ran forward, throwing my arms around his thick neck. "Are you okay?"

He grinned—apparently the bloodletting wasn't all that serious. "I had quite an adventure," he said. "I slid down a cliff, tangled with a few vampire bats, and nearly jumped out of my skin when I met a bobcat. But I'm here now. And apparently you were right about taking the road." His mood veered to seriousness. "Is Daniel all right?"

"He's at the hospital and Brenda's with him. Chad's with Señor Rodriguez, and I'm here, obviously, waiting for you."

Bright red rushed up from his collar and flooded his face. "That was nice of ya."

"Well—" I shrugged, not wanting him to read too much into it—"we couldn't go off and leave you out there with the vampire bats."

He slipped his arm around my shoulder as I led him toward the house. Señora Rodriguez saw us coming and started making clucking noises as she retreated to get her first-aid supplies.

"She's a sweetheart," I said. "Let her fix you up, then we'll go to the hospital to see Daniel. Brenda would probably appreciate seeing a few familiar faces about now."

"What's this?" Tank took my hand and caressed my bandaged thumb. "What happened?"

"Nasty little sucker tried to chew his way free when I was pulling him off Daniel," I said, shrugging. "Whoever called those things *fairies* had a twisted sense of humor."

"You should probably get a shot," Tank said, completely serious. "Rabies or tetanus, at least."

I blew out a breath. "I hate to admit it, but you're probably right."

* * *

The nearest hospital, we learned, was about an hour from the Rodriguez's farm, in a town called Morelos. We were halfway there when I remembered that our driver would go to the campsite to pick us up in a few hours, but we would no longer be at that spot. I found his number on my phone and was able to cancel our pickup. We weren't going back to Mexico City until Daniel was fit to travel, no matter how long it took.

We found Brenda and Daniel at a trauma center in the heart of the city. Daniel lay inside a curtained cubicle, awake and in such pain that tears streamed down his cheeks at a near-constant rate. His thin frame writhed on the mattress like a cut snake, and to make matters worse, the doctor insisted on keeping him flat on his stomach so they could have access to the stinger in his back.

An X-ray, Brenda told me, her face the color of ashes, had shown that the stinger had worked its way into Daniel's body, almost into the sheath around his spinal column. "I don't know what that thing is," she told me, steel in her voice, "but Daniel is in so much pain that I'm ready to strangle the next person who mentions fairies with my bare hands."

I slipped my arm around her shoulders and told her she should get some rest. "I can't," she said. "They have Daniel on a morphine drip, and even that isn't easing his pain. And the doctors keep quizzing me—they're driving me crazy."

"Quizzing you?"

"Oh, yeah." She looked at the ceiling and sighed, clearly exasperated. "They asked how a black woman came to have a white son. They asked why Daniel doesn't talk much. They asked what stung him—I told them I didn't know for sure, and I don't. They asked what we were doing out in the woods, and why we were in Mexico in the first place. I tried to give them as little information as possible, but I'd tell them anything if it would help Daniel."

"I know." I patted her shoulder again, then led her back to Daniel's cubicle and sat next to her. A nurse was in the cubicle checking Daniel's blood pressure, but she didn't interrupt us. She only smiled and went about her work.

Still, I lowered my voice when I spoke to Brenda. "I feel bad because we came all this way and went through all this, and for what? We still don't know what that thing is."

"But we know it's real," she said. "And we know it's dangerous."

"I didn't even see the stinger at first. I was so fascinated by the face and the wings."

Brenda grabbed my hands. "Andi, what am I gonna do if he doesn't get better?"

Tears welled in her eyes, and I didn't know what to do. So I hugged her, made a bunch of promises I couldn't keep, and found myself wishing that Tank would come around the corner. Even though he hadn't been able to heal Daniel, he was a calming influence, and we certainly could use one . . .

When Brenda finally pulled away, I noticed that the nurse had gone. While Brenda blew her nose and swiped at her eyes, I stood and moved to Daniel's bedside. His head was turned toward me, and I could see his eyes jumping beneath his paper-thin eyelids. The corner of his mouth twitched occasionally, and a muscle at his jaw kept tightening and relaxing, over and over . . .

"Excuse me." I looked up. The nurse had returned, this time without her clipboard. Instead she held a black book.

"Do you have news from the doctor?" Brenda asked, alarmed.

Tank and Chad chose that moment to join us, slipping into the cubicle behind the nurse. Tank nodded and smiled at her, but Chad narrowed his eyes. "Are you assigned to this case?" he asked, his voice curt. "If you're here to read the last rites or something—"

"Chad," I said gently. "Nurses do not administer the last rights." I looked at her. "Do you have news for us?"

A blush crossed the young woman's face. "*Con permiso*, I do not mean to bother you. But I have been overhearing things, and your words reminded me of this." She lifted the book.

"What's that?" Chad asked, practically snatching the book from the woman's grip. "*La Biblia de Estudio*," he read. "What's that?"

"I think," I said, "you should return the woman's study Bible."

He flushed and returned the book. "Sorry."

The nurse smiled.

"Go on," Tank said. "What did their conversation remind you of?"

I narrowed my gaze, wondering why he would encourage the nurse to take up our time with inane words from a centuries-old book, but Tank would listen to a toddler babble if he thought it would make the kid happy. Resigned, I turned back to Daniel, pressing my hand to his forehead. The boy was burning hot.

"*Este*," the nurse said. I heard the rustle of pages, then she began to read:

> The fifth angel sounded his shofar; and I saw a star that had fallen out of heaven onto the earth, and he was given the key to the shaft leading down to the Abyss. He opened the shaft of the Abyss, and there went up smoke from the shaft like the smoke of a huge furnace; the sun was darkened, and the sky too, by the smoke from the shaft. Then out of the smoke onto the earth came locusts, and they were given power like the power scorpions have on earth. They were instructed not to harm the grass on the earth, any green plant or any tree, but only the people who did not have the seal of God on their foreheads. The locusts were not

allowed to kill them, only to inflict pain on them for five months; and the pain they caused was like the pain of a scorpion sting. In those days people will seek death but will not find it; they will long to die, but death will elude them.

Now these locusts looked like horses outfitted for battle. On their heads were what looked like crowns of gold, and their faces were like human faces. They had hair like women's hair, and their teeth were like those of lions. Their chests were like iron breastplates, and the sound their wings made was like the roar of many horses and chariots rushing into battle. They had tails like those of scorpions, with stings; and in their tails was their power to hurt people for five months. They had as king over them the angel of the Abyss, whose name in Hebrew is *Abaddon* and in our language, *Destroyer*.

We had all been listening politely until we heard the words "tails like those of scorpions, with stings." I turned at that point, and Brenda looked at me, her eyes wide. Tank's mouth had fallen open, and though Chad seemed confused, he also seemed to understand that we had just stumbled over something important.

"Thank you," Tank said, placing one hand on the nurse's shoulder and gently guiding her out of the cubicle. "Thank you so much."

When he returned, he pulled the curtain closed, then crossed his arms and looked at me. "Remember what Dr. Wu said? Prototype."

I frowned. "You mean—"

"We know the Gate is doing genetic experiments, combining human DNA with strange DNA—maybe from aliens, maybe from other animals, who knows? But the two specimens in Prospero's office were different— version A and version B. They are working up to Version C, the one that will have—what did it say?—*chests like iron breastplates*."

"They already have teeth like lions," I pointed out, holding up my injured hand. "And when there are lots of them flying around, they could sound like chariots getting ready for battle."

"So they're not fairies," Chad said. "They're locusts."

"Not designed to mow down crops," Tank added. "But men."

Brenda looked at me. "Did you see more than the two at the camp?"

"Oh, yeah." I drew a deep breath. "While I was walking back to the farm, I saw a swarm of them coming from a spot at the edge of the woods. They took off when they saw me, and when I checked out the place where they were gathered, I saw a boulder with an opening in it."

"Like an abyss?" Tank lifted a brow.

"More like a cave," I said. "But I didn't have a chance to look around."

Tank nodded. "No matter where they come from, they're here. And that passage is from the book of Revelation. It's a record of the vision John saw when the Lord let him witness events of the last days. Apparently—if we're reading this right—the Gate is preparing something John saw more than two thousand years ago."

He leaned on the edge of Daniel's bed as a frown settled between his brows. "I don't get it, though. The plagues of the last days are part of God's judgment on the earth, a punishment for sin. How can those creatures be the result of the Gate's work if they are judgments from God? That'd be like terrorists making a bomb for New York City, but the United States stepping in and using it instead."

"You lost me a long time ago," Brenda said, bringing her hands to the sides of her face. "I don't get it and I never will."

"I get it," I said, the picture coming into focus for the first time. "Don't you see? It's brilliant! It's beautiful."

Tank's frown deepened. "What are you talkin' about?"

"HaShem." I nearly laughed aloud with the joy of discovery. "He is above all, right?"

Tank nodded.

"He is omnipotent—more powerful than any force, right?"

Tank nodded again.

"Then how like him to foil the machinations of evil people to suit his own purposes! You are exactly right, Tank—the Gate and whoever might make bombs and creatures and black-eyed children and flying spheres and malignant bacteria, but HaShem can and will thwart their purposes when He is ready. There's no contradiction. Instead, I see evidence of His power and purpose."

Tank tilted his head as a slow smile spread across his face. "Yeah. Yeah, I think I get it."

"I don't." Chad sat next to Brenda, slouching as he buried his hands in his pockets. "Are you planning to tell our bosses that these creatures are harmless because God wins in the end? Sounds a little pat."

"They're not harmless," I said. "Look at Daniel—he's proof that they're not harmless. As long as the Gate's people are testing prototypes, innocent people stand a good chance of being hurt. Just like the people who run into the black-eyed kids or who are infected by the deadly slime."

"The earth suffers, too," Brenda said, her gaze fastened to Daniel's face. "Remember the bird and fish kills? The dolphins that died from the green slime? The people we're fighting against are set on destruction. That's evil, pure and simple. And so is what they did to my boy."

"It is," I told her. "But you've gotta see the big picture, too. People will get hurt in skirmishes, but evil is not going to win the war."

Chapter 9

Two days later, the doctors at the trauma center said they were willing to discharge Daniel. They had extracted the stinger, sent it away to be tested at a lab ("I'd like to see those results," Chad quipped), and given Brenda a prescription for extra-strength pain killers. "But you must wean your son off the pills as soon as you can," the doctor warned. "You do not want to foster a dependency on drugs."

Brenda snorted. "Tell me something I don't know."

Brenda was signing papers and preparing for Daniel's discharge while I tried to keep track of our people, our luggage, and the proof we needed to submit to our bosses. Chad and Tank had called our driver and asked to go back to the campsite—to gather the video camera and anything else that might prove important.

I didn't think they'd find much. Maybe the desiccated body of the fairy that bit me and attacked Daniel, but I didn't think the body would last long in the tropical humidity.

While Brenda settled things with the hospital staff, I went to visit Daniel. The kid had been through so much in his life, it hardly seemed fair that he'd been the one to get stung. That fairy—that *imp*—had completely ignored me and Brenda and gone straight for Daniel. Did it *want* to torture a kid? Did it see Daniel as the most vulnerable, or did it sense that he had the ability to see into the spirit world and recognize them for the *duchs* they were . . .

"Hey, kiddo."

Daniel was sitting on the edge of his bed, dressed in new jeans and a new shirt. He grinned when I popped in, and slid off the mattress. "Can we go home now?"

"You bet. Your mom is signing papers, and Tank and Chad will be with us soon."

I'd just finished speaking when Tank lumbered into the room and dropped a big red sombrero on Daniel's head. "Gotcha souvenir," he said, grinning. "And Chad is waiting outside, ready to take you to your mom. Ready?"

"Ready!" Daniel ran outside to meet Chad. As Tank dropped into a chair, I listened to Daniel's chatter as it faded away.

I turned to Tank, but his sunny disposition had evaporated. He was no longer smiling—unusual for him—and he was massaging the skin at the bridge of his nose as if he had a headache.

"You okay?" I asked.

He nodded, then slowly shook his head from left to right. "Yeah," he finally said, opening his eyes, "and no. Yeah, there's nothing wrong with me. But no, because I'm struggling."

"With what?"

He blew out an explosive breath. "I know it's a universal hang-up. I know lots of people can't believe in God because of it. But I never thought I'd stumble over the same thing."

"Enough already." I tapped his hand. "I can't help if you won't explain yourself."

He hesitated, then placed his hand on top of mine. "Why does God allow good people to suffer?"

"Ohh." I sat next to him. "That question has tripped up all kinds of people. Why should you be immune?"

"Because I'm a believer. A strong believer, or so I thought. I know God's in charge, and I'm usually happy to let him be in charge, you know?"

I nodded. "So?"

"So when I looked at my little buddy in that bed—" His voice broke. "Why couldn't God have let that evil thing sting me?"

"Or Chad?" I suggested.

Tank barked a laugh. "Right. But . . . it didn't hurt us, it hurt Daniel. The weakest of us. The one who has already suffered the most."

"I know," I whispered.

"And then when I tried to heal him—God gave me a gift, you know, so why didn't it work when I tried to heal Daniel? If God could give me the power to bring a *dog* back to life, why couldn't he allow me to stop Daniel's pain?"

I shook my head, caught up in the awful memory of when Abby had been dead on the beach, killed by some horrible alien thing . . . but Tank had brought her back. Or HaShem had.

But I couldn't explain why sometimes Tank's gift failed any more than I could explain why sometimes I saw patterns and connections as clear as air and sometimes I only saw confusion . . . like now.

I sat quietly, respecting his confusion and knowing there were no easy answers. I sure didn't have any. Millions of other people had considered his question and come up empty.

But Tank was stronger than he realized. And wiser.

"I guess—" he lowered his head as if he were peering through a passageway filled with obstacles—"it's all a matter of faith, isn't it? We either trust that God knows what He's doing, or we think we know a better answer. Like letting that thing sting me—that'd be a better situation, wouldn't it? But God is good and He knows best, so He has a reason for my little buddy's pain . . . a reason I just can't see."

"Do you have to see it?"

He lifted a brow. "I'd *like* to see it, because then it would all make sense. But no, I guess I don't."

"Why not?"

"Because . . . God's got it covered, and I'm not God." He smiled, not the happy-go-lucky smile that was part of his nature, but a sadder, wiser version that made my heart ache.

Chapter 10

Chad and Tank had picked up the video camera from the website, but they had neglected to grab all the really important things. "Like my makeup kit," Brenda said, frowning as she searched her back pack. "How could you forget that?"

So before heading to the airport, we had our driver take us back to the campsite so we could grab anything we couldn't leave behind. I found my iPad beneath a sleeping bag, and Brenda found Daniel's video game by the window. And her makeup bag, of course.

We left the tent, lantern, and all that other stuff behind, though we told the driver he could come get it if he wanted to—if no one else beat him to it.

Once we boarded the private plane waiting to take us back to Dallas, I opened my iPad and took a good look around. I had to make a final report to the Watchers, and wanted it to be as complete as possible. We had returned with answers, video proof, and wisdom about the effects of the fairy-locusts, but we had paid a lot for those gains. Daniel had been traumatized, Brenda had suffered, and Tank's faith had been tested. This had not been an easy gig.

Reclining in one of the seats, Tank looked exhausted—not only from our adventure, but from the spiritual struggle he'd faced. I knew he'd come to terms with what happened to Daniel, but if he were God, he would have come up with an alternate plan.

Chad had actually been useful on this trip. He hadn't been able to help get us an ambulance (when I asked about his attempt to find help via a mind-to-mind connection, he said the only person he was able to contact was an old woman in Cleveland who thought she was talking to an angel). He had provided some interesting ideas, and, thanks to his cold meds, he'd actually dropped his snarky facade for a while. Tank still didn't seem very comfortable with the new guy, but he would adjust. We all would.

Brenda—one look at her face told me that she'd been through the wringer and back on this trip. Not only had the fairy freaked her out, but she'd taken Daniel's pain on herself, and her face reflected that agony. For the first time I could see wrinkles in her skin, deep worry lines in her forehead, and shadows beneath her eyes. She remained quiet on the plane, and that was unusual in itself.

And Daniel—the kid had been a trooper, considering all he'd been through. He was resting now, his head in Brenda's lap, a soft smile on his lips, as if he relished the gentle way her fingernails combed his hair. Poor kid. Considering all the years he spent in that psychiatric hospital, I'd bet he was way behind on his fair share of love taps and hair-ruffling. No wonder he lapped up affection the way a kitten laps up cream.

I plugged in my charger, synced my portable keyboard, and typed up a full report on my iPad. I tried not to leave out any important details, though I couldn't escape a niggling feeling that the Watchers already knew everything. I don't know how they would know, but the feeling persisted, all the same.

I also told our bosses about seeing the professor in the mirror before I found the mysterious folder.

None of us have ever heard of Ambrosi Giacomo, I

wrote, *but if the professor wanted me to have that information, it must be important. If it's a piece to our puzzle, we haven't found the place where it fits. But I'm sure we will.*

In the meantime, we will see what we can dig up on Mr. Giacomo. If you have any information you can share, please do. We need all the help we can get.

Thank you for the support on this mission. And if you can send another set of communications units, we'll try not to lose them.

Chapter 11

Back at the hotel, we walked through the lobby without speaking and went straight to the elevators. Something in our haggard appearance must have been alarming, because once we got into an empty elevator car, no one wanted to join us.

We rode up to the top floor, then stepped out into the lobby.

"I don't care what happens next," Brenda said, her arm firmly around Daniel's shoulder. "Daniel and I are going to our suite and puttin' out the 'do not disturb' sign. Even if there's a massive earthquake or somethin', don't call us."

"You've earned a rest," I told her. "Both of you."

Both Tank and Chad walked me to my door—an exercise in overkill, if ever there was one.

"Thanks, guy," I said, pressing my key to the card reader. "Get some rest, okay? And Chad—" he hesitated— "better find some cold medicine without side effects."

He laughed. "Will do."

They waited for me to open my door, then nodded at me, glared at each other, and went their separate ways.

Blowing out a breath, I stepped into the stillness of my room, dropped my bag in the entrance, and paused before the wall mirror in the hallway. I saw myself reflected there, along with the silk flowers on the foyer table and the wall behind me. Nothing else—no professor, no fairy, no creatures from the black lagoon.

For the moment, at least.

AUTHOR'S NOTE

¡Hola! Angie here, with two bits of information for you.

First, Al G. is fond of saying that if you have a 100,000 word manuscript and it is 99.9 percent perfect, you're still going to have 100 mistakes.

We try very hard to create perfect stories for you, but the occasional typo may slip by. If you spot one, you can help by writing us and telling us where and what it is. We'd love to make it right.

So if you find one of those pesky typos, please write us at harbingers777@gmail.com. We will quickly put it out of its misery.

Second, I have always thought that the best fiction is based on fact. My delight lies in taking what is real and exploring possibilities. The fish and bird deaths I featured in *Sentinels* are actually happening. The black-eyed children I featured in *Hybrids* have been reported around the world. And now: fairies.

In the summer of 2016, I was finishing up a historical novel when I learned about something my friend L.A. Marzulli had discovered. His exploration of "the fairy" caught my attention, and the possibilities naturally lent themselves to a Harbingers adventure.

If you would like to see video of the actual creature, visit L.A.'s blog at this link: https://lamarzulli.wordpress.com/tag/watchers-10/

I would also love to share a chapter from L.A.'s latest book, *Nephilim Hybrids*. It contains an interview between L.A. and a veterinarian who examined the actual X-rays of "the fairy."

FROM L.A. MARZULLI

The "Winged Nightmare" or, as Richard Shaw calls it, "The Fairy," has been controversial to say the least.

As we are getting ready to go to press, Jaime Mausson gave me the X-rays of the winged creature. I had them mounted and presented them, along with other pictures, to a veterinarian who wishes to remain anonymous.

(I have found that many people are reluctant to officially come on the record because of the fear of ridicule.)

The vet looked at the creature and this is what he said:

L.A.: So...we're looking at the wing structure where the wings actually attach themselves to the creature. Can you speak to that, please?

Vet: Yes, I'm looking at the X-rays, the radio-opaque structure that wings attach to. They appear to be some sort of bone and it looks like the thin bones that hold the wing structure together are fused very nicely to whatever that structure is. I assume it's a bone. It looks like they're fused in there naturally, as opposed to someone slopping it together. The only problem is that it's almost too opaque. It doesn't match up with the radiodensity of the other bones.

L.A.: Yes, but wouldn't having a creature like this with the wings protruding from the back, wouldn't there have to be some kind of anchoring to the skeletal structure? Wouldn't the bone be thicker there?

Vet: Yes, it's very possible—could be if this is a flying creature.

L.A.: Which it is.

Vet: For example, chickens [and] birds are going to have a lot less radiodensity in their other bones; in their legs and those bones are more hollow compared to, say, mammal bones. So these bones up here—that hold the wings—could be a little more thick and radiodense and calcified because it needs more stability to keep the wings attached.

L.A.: In your opinion, looking at the pictures and X-rays we've been looking at . . . could this be some sort of a composite, based on four or five different animals? Look at the face and the teeth and the ears. What are your thoughts?

Vet: If it is, it's a very, very good composite. Someone very professional put this thing together. I mean just the way the bones... I can see the joints; I can see where the ribs lead into the sternum. I can see the femur, going into the hip. For someone to put this together would require a lot of work.

L.A.: And for what reason? No one's making any money off this. It's not on the cover of the *National Enquirer* or something, selling millions of papers. That's not the case here. This thing has been in formaldehyde for three or four years.

Vet: I suppose anything's possible. If it's a fake, someone put a lot of work into this to put this together. I can't think of an animal that you could add stuff on too. Very odd.

L.A.: Very unsettling. When we saw it, we were speechless.

Vet: Whatever this is that's trying to hold this fracture together in the tibia [the leg]. For someone to think ahead of time ... How would you know where the fracture was, unless you were some sort of medical professional? How did you get that stuff that's holding that fracture together under the skin? It's not an easy job.

L.A.: How would you do that?

Vet: Yeah, that's not an easy job to do, to get that under the skin even though it's not in the right spot.

L.A.: It's a classic gargoyle. It's evil to say the least. Again, when we saw it, it was unsettling. Look at the way the wings are attached. I mean, anatomically it's very proportional isn't it?

Vet: Yes. I don't see the teeth in the back of the jaw...

L.A.: What would be your take away?

Vet: From a medical standpoint, these are real

bones, real joints, and real X-rays. The question is, what kind of animal is it? And if it is a fake, what animals did they use to put this together? It would be a very professional job if it was a fake. You need to get a forensic pathologist, because I'm just looking at some X-rays. They look like real X-rays to me.

L.A.: Closing thoughts?

Vet: I'm perplexed about these round objects in the X-ray.

L.A.: We are, too. Any idea what that might be?

Vet: Perhaps someone shot it with a BB-gun and that's how it died…

L.A.: So you think these round things are metal?

Vet: They look like metal. If I had to guess, metal objects round like this . . . I've seen this before; in animals it's pretty clear. BBs, it could be buckshot. A shotgun. Buck-shot. Someone mistook it for a bird or something.

L.A.: Ah. Ok. That's interesting. Buck-shot. That would really make a lot of sense.

Vet: It's a far away shot.

L.A.: Yes. Wow. Interesting.

Vet: The shot may have broken the bone [in the leg].

L.A.: Thank you for coming on the record with us.

Vet: Nice to meet you.

Summation by L.A. Marzulli:

So as of June 2016, I will state that I believe the Winged Nightmare is not a hoax and that is the real thing. The fact that the vet was able to state that he believed the BB-like balls showing up in the X-ray were the result of buckshot or bird shot solves a lot of what perplexed us for some time.

In other words, this creature may have been blasted out of the sky by someone with a shotgun.

This explains the broken leg and the BB's randomly placed throughout the body.

More testing needs to be done and I'll be giving updates as they come to us.

We are now in the process of trying to get the creature out of Mexico legally so that extensive DNA testing can be done in the States.

L.A. Marzulli
June 2016

Sneak Peek at Harbingers 16
At Sea
Alton Gansky

Rocking.

Like an infant in a cradle.

Gentle. Smooth. Even.

Then came a new sensation: Someone had been using my mouth as an ashtray. A vile film covered my tongue and teeth. Still, I wasn't ready to open my eyes. Mostly I just wanted to slip back into the blanket of sleep I had been living in a short time before.

Blanket? I could tell I lay upon a narrow bed, but I felt no blanket over me. I was warm. Too warm. Only then did I risk opening an eye. The room was lit but only dimly. Missing was the harshness of an incandescent light. What I saw was natural illumination, enough to see but not read comfortably.

I forced myself to take several deep breaths. The air was a tad stale and carried a hint of salt. I swung my legs over the side of the bed, buried my face in my hands and tried to focus my thoughts. It wasn't easy. My brain was filled with a thick London fog and my thoughts were as slippery as a sink full of eels.

Lowering my hands, I stared at the thin carpet on the floor. It was a perfectly acceptable beige, which somehow managed to look new and old at the same time. My brain fog lifted a little and I was capable of noticing something that shouldn't be: black, highly polished dress shoes. The kind of shoes a man wore with a—

Tux.

Sure enough, I wore a pair of well-tailored tuxedo pants. I stood and touched my waist. Cummerbund. There was also a white shirt with posts instead of buttons, and a bowtie. I had been sleeping in a bowtie. The thing is, I hate tuxes. At least I think I do. Try as I might, I couldn't remember the last time I wore a tux, or why I was wearing one now.

Across the room was a full length mirror that confirmed everything I had just discovered. I didn't need a mirror to tell me what I was wearing. I puzzled that out pretty quickly. What I *did* need was a mirror or something else to tell me who the guy in the reflection was. He looked familiar. Young and big. Extra big. A little wide in the shoulders too. I stepped closer to the mirror and touched its cool, smooth surface. The reflection touched its side of the glass.

A man should recognize his own image shouldn't he? Why then couldn't I recognize mine?

My first question had been: Why am I sleeping in a tuxedo? That seemed like a small question now. What I really wanted to know was who I am. I also wouldn't mind knowing where I was. I didn't recognize anything in the cramped room.

"Well, this ain't right." At least my voice sounded familiar.

Don't miss the other books in the Harbingers series which can be purchased separately or in collections:

CYCLE ONE: INVITATION
The Call
The House
The Sentinels
The Girl

CYCLE TWO: MOSAIC
The Revealing
Infestation
Infiltration
The Fog

CYCLE THREE: THE PROBING
Leviathan
The Mind Pirates
Hybrids
The Village

Selected Books by Angela Hunt

Roanoke
Jamestown
Hartford
Rehoboth
Charles Towne
Magdalene
The Novelist
Uncharted
The Awakening
The Debt
The Elevator
The Face
Let Darkness Come
Unspoken
The Justice
The Note
The Immortal
The Truth Teller
The Silver Sword

The Golden Cross
The Velvet Shadow
The Emerald Isle
Dreamers
Brothers
Journey
Doesn't She Look Natural?
She Always Wore Red
She's In a Better Place
Five Miles South of Peculiar
The Fine Art of Insincerity
The Offering
Esther: Royal Beauty
Bathsheba: Reluctant Beauty
RISEN

Web page: www.angelahuntbooks.com

Facebook:
https://www.facebook.com/angela.e.hunt

FAIRY

61362074R00064

Made in the USA
Charleston, SC
21 September 2016